Elizabeth blinked at him in confusion. "What?"

"Do you have a boyfriend?"

"There was," she said quietly, then sighed and turned back to meet his gaze. "But not any longer."

Relief washed through Woodrow in waves. Pushing off the porch, he stood and drew her up to stand opposite him. "Good. Because I sure wouldn't want someone to come gunning for me."

"Why would anyone come—"

Before she could finish the question, he slipped his arms around her waist and pulled her hips to him. As her gaze met his, he saw the passion that smoked her eyes, as well as the wonder. "Doc?"

"Yes?"

"Last night I slept with you. Held you. I can't do that tonight. Not without making love with you."

Dear Reader,

Thank you for choosing Silhouette Desire—where passion is guaranteed in every read. Things sure are heating up with our continuing series DYNASTIES: THE BARONES. Eileen Wilks's *With Private Eyes* is a powerful romance that helps set the stage for the daring conclusion next month. And if it's more continuing stories that you want— we have them. TEXAS CATTLEMAN'S CLUB: THE STOLEN BABY launches this month with Sara Orwig's *Entangled with a Texan*.

The wonderful Peggy Moreland is on hand to dish up her share of Texas humor and heat with *Baby, You're Mine*, the next installment of her TANNERS OF TEXAS series. Be sure to catch Peggy's Silhouette Single Title, *Tanner's Millions*, on sale January 2004. Award-winning author Jennifer Greene marks her much-anticipated return to Silhouette Desire with *Wild in the Field*, the first book in her series THE SCENT OF LAVENDER.

Also for your enjoyment this month, we offer Katherine Garbera's second book in the KING OF HEARTS series. *Cinderella's Christmas Affair* is a fabulous "it could happen to you" plot guaranteed to leave her fans extremely satisfied. And rounding out our selection of delectable stories is *Awakening Beauty* by Amy J. Fetzer, a steamy, sensational tale.

More passion to you!

Melissa Jeglinski

Melissa Jeglinski
Senior Editor, Silhouette Desire

Please address questions and book requests to:
Silhouette Reader Service
U.S.: 3010 Walden Ave., P.O. Box 1325, Buffalo, NY 14269
Canadian: P.O. Box 609, Fort Erie, Ont. L2A 5X3

Baby, You're Mine

PEGGY MORELAND

Published by Silhouette Books

America's Publisher of Contemporary Romance

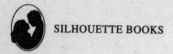

SILHOUETTE BOOKS

ISBN 0-373-76544-4

BABY, YOU'RE MINE

Books by Peggy Moreland

Silhouette Desire

A Little Bit Country #515
Run for the Roses #598
Miss Prim #682
The Rescuer #765
Seven Year Itch #837
The Baby Doctor #867
Miss Lizzy's Legacy #921
A Willful Marriage #1024
*Marry Me, Cowboy #1084
*A Little Texas Two-Step #1090
*Lone Star Kind of Man #1096
†*The Rancher's Spittin'*
   Image #1156
†*The Restless Virgin* #1163
†*A Sparkle in the Cowboy's Eyes* #1168

†*That McCloud Woman* #1227
Billionaire Bridegroom #1244
†*Hard Lovin' Man* #1270
‡*Ride a Wild Heart* #1306
‡*In Name Only* #1313
‡*Slow Waltz Across Texas* #1315
Groom of Fortune #1336
The Way to a Rancher's
   Heart #1345
Millionaire Boss #1365
The Texan's Tiny Secret #1394
Her Lone Star Protector #1426
**Five Brothers and a Baby #1532
**Baby, You're Mine #1544

Silhouette Special Edition

Rugrats and Rawhide #1084

*Trouble in Texas
†Texas Brides
‡Texas Grooms
**The Tanners of Texas

Silhouette Books

Turning Point 2002
"It Had To Be You"

To the One I Love 2003
"Caught by a Cowboy"

PEGGY MORELAND

published her first romance with Silhouette in 1989 and continues to delight readers with stories set in her home state of Texas. Winner of the National Readers' Choice Award, a nominee for the *Romantic Times* Reviewer's Choice Award and a two-time finalist for the prestigious RITA® Award, Peggy has frequently appeared on the *USA TODAY* and Waldenbooks's bestseller lists. When not writing, you can usually find Peggy outside, tending the cattle, goats and other critters on the ranch she shares with her husband. You may write to Peggy at P.O. Box 1099, Florence, TX 76527-1099, or e-mail her at peggy@peggymoreland.com.

One

Cantankerous. That's what polite folks called Woodrow Tanner. Less courteous ones used a riper, more colorful word, one not often used in the presence of women or within hearing distance of the preacher. But Woodrow didn't give a tinker's damn what people called him and less what they thought of him as a person. He did as he damn well pleased and to hell with anyone who disapproved.

He owned seven hundred and fifty acres of prime ranch land southwest of Tanner's Crossing and lived in a log house he'd built dead-center in the property. He'd placed it there for the sole purpose of putting as much distance as possible from himself and his neighbors. Other than a blue-heeler dog that insisted on sleeping at the foot of his bed, he lived alone and planned to keep it that way. His biggest beefs in life—and the ones sure to put him in a bad mood— were large crowds, big cities and traffic jams that consisted of anything more than a couple of farm trucks trapped behind a slow-moving tractor. Since he was currently crawling at a snail's pace down Dallas, Texas's Central Expressway, his normal cantankerous mood was registering on the dangerous side of the scale.

If his brother Ace had been within grabbing distance, he would've gladly blacked one of his eyes, maybe even bloodied his nose, for sending him on this wild goose chase. Not that Woodrow had willingly accepted the assignment. He'd cussed and kicked aplenty, demanding that one of the other Tanner brothers make the trip instead. But Ace had sworn that Woodrow was the only one available, claiming that Ry couldn't spare the time from his surgical practice, and Rory was out of town, buying the next season's goods for his chain of country western stores. Ace hadn't offered an excuse for Whit and Woodrow hadn't bothered to ask for one. Whit's stepbrother status exempted him from most family obligations, an immunity that Woodrow resented more than a little.

So, in the end, it was Woodrow who was elected to travel to Dallas to take care of a little family business.

But that didn't mean he had to like it.

Ahead, he saw his exit and bullied his dually truck into the far right lane. Once free of the expressway and the cars clogging it, he relaxed a little and checked his directions again. Two more rights and a left and he was pulling into a parking space in front of a modern, five-story building. He shuddered at all the metal and glass towering before him. Personally he preferred natural materials. Stone. Wood. Brick was all right if used to construct a commercial building, such as a post office or a bank. But anything beyond those three materials, he considered a defamation to the landscape, an eyesore, something better suited for someplace like, say…Mars.

With his mood growing darker by the minute, he climbed from his truck and headed for the building's entrance. Once inside, he checked the directory, then took the elevator to the fifth floor. He found the door marked Elizabeth Montgomery, Pediatrician, and pushed it open. Without a glance to either side, he strode straight for the reception window and rapped his knuckles against the glass.

A woman glanced up from her work, then higher, until her gaze met his. Her eyes widened and her jaw sagged. Woodrow was accustomed to the reaction. The Tanner men were known for their size and their looks and generally created a stir with women, intended or not.

Slowly the woman stood and rolled back the window. ''Can I help you?''

''Yeah. I need to see Dr. Montgomery.''

She leaned to peer around him, as if she expected to find someone hiding behind him. Someone decidedly smaller. ''Do you have an appointment?''

''No. This is personal.''

Her brows drew together. "Is the doctor expecting you?"

"No."

"If you'll give me your name, I'll tell her you're here."

"Woodrow Tanner."

She took a step back, her wide-eyed gaze fixed on his. "Wait just a minute. I'll be right back."

Woodrow watched her whirl and all but run down the hall. At the end, she rapped sharply on a door, then opened it and slipped inside. Scowling, he braced his wide hands on the countertop and drummed his fingers while he waited.

Moments later, the woman reappeared. She paused to fluff her hair and tug down the hem of her uniform's top, before starting back down the hallway toward him. He couldn't help but notice the swing she'd added to her hips' movement on the return trip.

When she reached the reception desk, she leaned close to the window. "I'm sorry," she said, her voice having turned sultry on the return trip, "but Dr. Montgomery's schedule is full today." She lifted a hand to toy with the top button of her uniform's top and batted her eyes at him. "But if you'd like, I can make an appointment for you to see her."

Unless he was mistaken—and he could be, since he was a little out of practice—the woman was flirting with him. Another day, another *place* and he might've flirted right back. But, as it was, nothing, not even a hand-engraved invitation for a quick roll in the hay, could persuade him to spend another minute longer than necessary in Dallas, Texas.

"What time do y'all lock up for the day?" he asked.

Her smile brightened a notch or two. "Four o'clock."

It was obvious she thought he was asking the question to find out what time she'd be free. He didn't bother to set her straight. He figured any misunderstanding was hers to deal with, not his.

He glanced at his watch and noted that it was half past three. "I'll wait."

She fluttered a hand toward the waiting room. "Just have a seat over there. Can I get you something to drink?"

Already turning away, Woodrow shook his head, sure that the offer didn't include a shot of whiskey.

And whiskey was what he needed right now.

Wedged in a chair better suited for one of the seven dwarfs, Woodrow considered passing the time by thumbing through one of the magazines scattered across the coffee table. But a closer inspection revealed titles like *Good Housekeeping, Working Mother* and *Ladies Home Journal,* and nothing, not even the threat of a hot branding iron on the hip, could persuade him to touch a one of them. Resigned to boredom, he tilted his head back against the wall and closed his eyes. Two breaths later, he was asleep.

"You'll need to call the lab and check on the results for the Carter baby. They promised to have it by Monday at four.''

Woodrow snapped up his head, blinked. A woman was standing in the doorway that separated the waiting area from the examining rooms. She had her hand braced against the door to hold it open and was talking to the receptionist, giving what sounded like last-minute instructions.

Must be the doc, he decided, noting the white lab coat, the stethoscope clasped around her throat like a necklace. Fully awake now, he narrowed his eyes and studied her profile.

She didn't look like a doctor, he decided. She looked more like somebody's spinster aunt. The horn-rimmed glasses were his first clue. The bun she'd swept her blond hair up in was the second. But then she turned her back fully to him and exposed the nape of a long graceful neck, and he was suddenly struck by the strongest urge to have his mouth there. Little wisps of hair curled against porcelain-smooth skin shades lighter than his own. Halfway between the collar of the lab coat she wore and the base of her hairline lay a tiny patch of pinker flesh.

A birthmark? he wondered. Nerves? A heat rash?

Whatever it was, it was on that spot that he wanted to center his mouth.

''Dr. Silsby will be taking my calls,'' he heard the doc say, and made himself focus on the conversation again. ''I've left the number where I can be reached on my desk, in the event of an emergency. And, of course, I'll have my pager with me.''

Woodrow straightened, his gut clenching. The doc was leaving town? He glanced at the receptionist, and she shot him a surreptitious wink. Knowing he'd best slip out before the receptionist boogered up his one chance of catching the doctor, he eased to his feet and slipped out the door. At the bank of elevators, he paused, hoping to corner the doc there on her way down.

Seconds later he heard the office door open and stole a glance that way. The doc was walking toward him, her head bent as she dug through a purse that hung from a slim shoulder.

He punched the Down button and the door opened. He slapped a hand against it and stepped to the side. "Going down?" he asked.

She glanced up, startled, as if unaware of his presence until that moment. "Why…yes. Thank you."

She pulled a key ring from her purse, then let the bag fall to swing at her side as she slipped past him. Woodrow released the door and stepped in after her. "First floor?"

"Yes, please," she replied, then shifted her gaze to watch the panel of lights that would mark their descent.

He punched the button, then moved to stand beside her. She took a discreet step to the side, keeping a safe distance from him. Cautious, he decided. Probably wise, since she lived in a big city like Dallas. As the car slowly descended, her scent drifted his way. That clean, sterile scent associated with doctors' offices and, beneath it, just a hint of something floral, more feminine.

When they reached the first floor, he placed a hand against the door and stepped back, permitting her to exit first.

Averting her gaze, she murmured, "Thank you," and swept past him.

He caught up with her in two strides, then slowed and matched his step to hers. "Are you Dr. Elizabeth Montgomery?"

She tightened her fingers on her purse strap, but she didn't look his way or slow. "Yes."

They reached the front entrance and Woodrow held the door open for her. Again, she murmured her thanks and swept past him, without making eye contact.

Frustrated, he strode after her. "If you've got a minute, I'd like to talk to you."

"I'm sorry. I'm running rather late, as it is."

She reached a car, a Mercedes, and fumbled with the automated lock on her key ring. He noticed that her fingers were shaking.

"I'm not a mugger," he said, hoping to put her fears at rest. "I just want to ask you a few questions."

She managed to unlock the door and slip inside. "As I said, I'm running late. Now, if you'll excuse me."

Woodrow caught the door before she could shut it in his face. "About your sister," he added pointedly.

She looked at him then, her blue eyes sharpening

behind the horn-rimmed glasses. "You know my sister?"

He stepped around the door and braced a hand along its top. "No. Not personally."

She gulped and turned her face away to stare through the windshield, her skin paler now, the knuckles on the hand she gripped the steering wheel with a pearly white. "I haven't seen her in years. She—" She clamped her lips together and angled her head, her eyes narrowed in suspicion. "Did she send you? Is she in trouble again?"

Woodrow blew out a long breath, unsure how best to proceed. "No. Well," he amended, frowning, "I wouldn't call it trouble exactly."

"If it's money she wants," she told him coolly, "you can tell her she can come and ask for it herself."

"No, ma'am," he said, growing more uncomfortable by the minute. "She doesn't need your money."

"Well, what does she want?" she snapped impatiently. "That's usually why she contacts me."

"Well…she…she…" He scowled, trying to think of a gentler way to deliver the news. Unable to think of anything, other than the bald truth, he muttered glumly, "Ma'am, your sister is dead."

The blood drained from her face. "Dead? My sister is *dead?*"

His expression grim, he gave his chin a jerk. "Yeah. A little over a month ago."

She pressed her fingers against her lips. "Dead," she said again.

Woodrow saw that her chin was trembling, watched the slow swell of tears in her eyes. "Yeah. You see, Star, she—"

She whipped her head around. "Star? My sister's name isn't Star. It's Renee. Renee Montgomery." Weak with relief, she dropped her forehead against the steering wheel. "Oh, thank God. For a minute there, I thought Renee was—" She stopped mid-sentence, then jerked up her head and pressed her lips tightly together. "I'm sorry," she said as she pushed the key into the ignition. "Obviously, you've made a mistake. Now, I really must be going."

When she reached for the door again, Woodrow blocked her way. "Wait." He dug the picture Ace had given him from his pocket and held it out. "Is this your sister?"

She pushed his hand away without so much as a glance. "I'm sorry. Really I am. But obviously you've made a mistake. My sister's name is Renee, not Star."

He thrust the picture in front of her face. "Just take a look."

She gave him an impatient look, then snatched the picture from his hand and held it at arm's length in order to better see it. Woodrow watched her facial muscles go slack, saw the tremble that began in her fingers.

She shook her head. "I don't understand." She turned to look at him, her eyes round with disbelief. "Where did you get this?"

"Maggie Dean. Maggie Tanner now, since she and my brother Ace got married. She worked with Star."

"Not Star," she told him and lifted the picture to look at it again. She placed a hand at the base of her throat and rubbed. "Renee. Renee Montgomery."

Woodrow hunkered down beside the car, putting himself on her level. "Look," he said quietly. "I know this has probably come as a shock, and I'm sorry that I had to dump this on you so unexpectedly, but there's more."

"More?" she repeated, then laughed, the sound hollow and empty to his ears. "What more could you possibly have to tell me, other than my sister is dead?"

Woodrow shifted on the balls of his feet, knowing he had to handle this carefully. Not for himself so much as for Ace and Maggie. "Well," he began. "You see, Star, I mean Renee," he corrected. "Well, she had a baby."

She stared. "A baby?"

He nodded. "Yeah. A girl."

"But…where is she?"

"With Ace and Maggie. Before Renee died, she made Maggie promise that she'd give the baby to the baby's father."

"Ace is the father of my sister's child?"

Woodrow blew out a long breath. This was getting tougher, instead of easier. "No. Not Ace. Ace's father. *Our* father," he clarified, scowling. "Buck Tanner. He fathered the kid."

She pressed two fingers to her temple, as if pushing

back a headache. "But why does Ace have the baby and not your father?"

"Because my father's dead. Heart attack. Just a couple of days after Renee died."

She leaned her head back against the seat and closed her eyes. "I can't believe this," she whispered. "Any of it."

"It's the truth," Woodrow assured her. "Every last word. I swear."

She sat there as still as death, not saying a word. Knowing it was now or never, he scooted closer. "We're still wrangling with all the legal stuff. Ace hired a private detective to track down Renee's family, which is how we found out about you. Ace and Maggie, they want to adopt the baby. That's why I'm here. To get your approval."

She dropped her chin, shaking her head. "No." She gulped. "I can't talk about this right now. It's too much to absorb. Too fast. I need time to think." She covered her face with her hands. "Oh, God. Renee."

Though time was the last thing Woodrow wanted to give her, he pushed to his feet. "I'll be staying in town overnight." He fished a gas receipt from his pocket and scrawled a number on the back. "Here's my cell phone number," he said, and tossed the paper onto her lap. "Give me a call, when you're ready to talk."

Still numb from learning of her sister's death, that evening Elizabeth stood before her breakfast room window, her arms hugged around her waist. Beyond the glass a hummingbird flitted from bloom to bloom in the garden, seeking nectar, while two squirrels played chase along the top rail of her wrought-iron fence. Behind her, Ted Scott, her fiancé, sat at her kitchen table. Though she couldn't see his face, she sensed his disapproval. It pressed down on her shoulders like a heavy cloak, adding to the sorrow already weighing her down.

"I know you're upset," he said, in a obvious struggle for patience. "I can understand that. But it would be ridiculous for us to cancel our trip now. Not after all the plans we've made. Besides, it isn't as if you have a funeral to arrange or anything. That's all been done."

Tears swelled in Elizabeth's eyes at the mention of the funeral. She'd lost her sister and hadn't even been allowed at the funeral to mourn her passing. Didn't even know where Renee had been buried or who had made the arrangements.

Oh, God, she wanted to cry so badly. Wanted to empty her heart and soul of all the grief and regrets that choked her. She squeezed her eyes shut and silently willed Ted to come to her. To wrap his arms around her and just hold her. Comfort her. Just once she wanted him to respond to her emotional needs, instead of stifling them.

When he remained at the table, she pushed back the disappointment and shook her head. "It doesn't matter. I need to stay here. Decide what to do."

"About the baby?"

She nodded, still unable to believe that Renee, little more than a baby herself, had been a mother.

And Elizabeth was an aunt.

"Surely you aren't considering adopting this child?" he said in dismay. "Why, it could be deformed, retarded! You told me yourself that Renee had taken drugs."

His callous words scraped across her heart, opening wounds scarred by the past. Slowly she turned to face him, her face white, her eyes fierce. "Do you think that matters to me, Ted? I have a niece. A *niece*. That baby is all the family I have left in the world. I won't just sign away whatever rights I may have to her and pretend she never existed."

Immediately contrite, he rose and crossed to slip his arms around her waist. "I'm sorry, Elizabeth," he murmured against her hair. "I wasn't thinking. Of course, you feel a responsibility for the baby. That's only natural. But you mustn't do anything rash. It wouldn't be wise. You're in shock, I'm sure. A week away will help. It'll give you the time to adjust to your loss, to put things in proper perspective."

She buried her face in the curve of his neck, clinging to him, desperate for his comfort, his understanding. But as tight as she clung, she felt nothing from him. No warmth. No understanding. Certainly no comfort. Just the stiffness of his starched collar chafing against her skin, the rigidity of his body where it touched hers.

Disheartened, she shook her head. "I can't go with you, Ted. Not now."

He dropped his arms from around her so quickly, she stumbled, off balance.

"Fine." He plucked his suit jacket from the back of the kitchen chair. "But if you think I'm going to stay here and hold your hand while you cry over a sister whom you haven't seen or spoken to in years, then you're mistaken. I'm going to Europe, with or without you."

"Then you'll want to take this with you." Tears burning her eyes, Elizabeth twisted her engagement ring from her finger and held it out to him.

He looked at the ring then back at her. His eyes turned cold, unforgiving. Snatching the ring from her hand, he rammed it into his pocket and spun for the door.

Elizabeth released the breath she'd been holding when the door slammed behind him. Crossing to it, she spun the lock, then turned her back to the door and buried her face in her hands.

"Yeah," Woodrow said wearily. "I'm still in Dallas." Holding the cell phone to his ear, he moved to the window in his hotel room to look down at the traffic below. Almost seven o'clock and the streets were still jammed with cars. Wondering why any one would choose to live such a rat-race existence, he warned his brother, "But not for much longer."

"Did you talk to her?"

Woodrow frowned and turned from the window. "Yeah. I talked to her. Didn't get very far, though."

"Is she going to fight us for custody of the baby?"

"Don't know. She said it was too much to deal with all at once. She needed time to think."

"That doesn't surprise me," Ace replied, his voice grim. "I'm sure it was a shock to learn her sister had died and left a newborn infant behind."

Woodrow remembered the shocked look on the doctor's face. But where was the grief? The hysterical female he'd expected to have to console? "Yeah," he agreed vaguely. "It was a shock all right."

"So when do you plan to talk with her again?"

"The ball's in her court now. I left her my cell number."

"You're just going to sit around and wait for her to call you?"

"What the hell do you want me to do?" Woodrow snapped impatiently. "Put a gun to her head and demand that she sign away her rights to the kid so you and Maggie can play mommy and daddy?" He immediately regretted the cruel remark, knowing how much his brother and sister-in-law loved that kid. He dragged a hand over his head. "I didn't mean that," he said wearily. "I'm just in a bad mood. You know how much I hate big cities."

"Yeah, I know, which is why I appreciate even more you doing this for us."

Woodrow grunted. "Yeah. Like I had a choice."

"Bring her here."

Woodrow pressed the phone closer to his ear, sure that he'd misunderstood. "What?"

"Bring Star's sister to the ranch. I'm sure she isn't going to feel comfortable releasing custody of her niece to complete strangers. Bring her here and let her get to know us. Let her see what ordinary people we are.''

''Ordinary?'' Woodrow repeated, then snorted a laugh. ''Brother, there's nothing ordinary about the Tanner family. We live from one scandal to the next, without time to catch our breaths before we're hit with another one.''

Elizabeth nervously fingered the piece of paper she'd slipped into her robe pocket. Scrawled on the back was Woodrow Tanner's cell phone number. He'd said for her to call him when she was ready to talk, though she was sure he'd meant when she had decided what she wanted to do about the custody issue. Unfortunately, in the hours since she'd learned of her sister's death, she hadn't reached a decision.

But she did have questions. Hundreds of them. How had Renee died? Was she alone when she passed away? How old was her baby? Did the baby look like Renee? Why hadn't Woodrow's father married Renee? Where had Renee lived? Where had she worked? Where was she buried? Had Renee never mentioned having a family? Was that why the Tanners had hired a private detective to track Elizabeth down?

She pulled the paper from her pocket and stared at the number. He'd have the answers, she told herself, and picked up the phone. She quickly punched in the number, then waited, telling herself that once she had answers, she'd have a clearer idea of what she should do about Renee's baby.

"Yo."

She jumped at the unexpected, gruff greeting. "Mr. Tanner?" she said uncertainly.

"Yeah."

"Um…this is Dr. Elizabeth Montgomery."

"Yeah, I know. I've got one of those fancy phones with caller ID. Even tells me the time. It's 1:33 a.m., in case you're wondering."

She winced, not having realized the hour. "I'm sorry. Really. I had no idea it was so late. I'll call back in the morning."

"No need. I wasn't asleep."

"Oh." She pressed a hand against the top of her head and began to pace. "Well, I've been thinking, Mr. Tanner—"

"Woodrow."

She stopped and frowned. "What?"

"Woodrow. That's my name."

"Oh." She sighed and dropped her hand. "Well, I've been thinking…Woodrow," she said cautiously, testing the sound of his name, "about what you said this afternoon. Concerning the custody," she clarified, and began to pace again. "I was hoping you might answer some questions for me."

"You wouldn't happen to have a pot of coffee made, would you?"

She stopped, wrinkling her brow in confusion. "What?"

"Coffee. You know. That black stuff."

"Well…no. Why?"

"Put some on. I think better after I've had a few cups."

"You're coming to my house?"

"I'm already here."

She whirled to stare at the front door. "You're *here?*" she repeated in dismay.

"Yeah. And when you open the door, would you mind giving the old bat across the street a wave? She's been watching me like a hawk. Probably thinks I'm a burglar."

Elizabeth hurried to the door and unlocked it. By the time she opened it, Woodrow was halfway up the walk, his cell phone still pressed to his ear. She stared, struck again by his size. She remembered thinking that afternoon how large a man he was, but he seemed even taller now, broader. And there was a John Wayne swagger in his walk that she hadn't noticed that afternoon, which made him appear even bigger, tougher.

"Wave," he said into the receiver.

She glanced beyond him and saw her neighbor, Mrs. Gladstone, peeking through a slit in the drapes of her front window. Forcing a smile, she lifted a hand in a wave.

"Is she still looking?" he asked.

Elizabeth watched Mrs. Gladstone snatch the drapes together and disappear. She tipped the receiver back to her mouth. "No. She's gone now."

"Good."

Reaching the porch, he slid his cell phone into the holster clipped to his belt, then pulled hers from her ear and punched the disconnect button. He passed it back to her. "I guess we don't need these anymore."

Her face heating in embarrassment, Elizabeth slipped the phone into the pocket of her robe. "No, I guess not."

He lifted a brow. "Are you going to invite me in?"

Flustered, she backed into the house. "Oh. Yes. Please." She waited for him to step inside, then closed and locked the door behind him.

"Nice place you've got here."

She turned, following his gaze, caught off guard by the comment. "Thank you. I like it."

He cupped a hand on her elbow. "Now, about that coffee…"

She stumbled along at his side, wondering belatedly if she'd made a mistake in inviting him in. After all, she knew nothing about this man. He could be a serial killer for all she knew.

"Mr. Tanner—"

They reached the kitchen and he released her arm. "Woodrow."

She squared her shoulders. "Woodrow," she amended. "May I see your driver's license, please?"

He gave her a curious look, but reached behind him and pulled his wallet from his rear pocket. "I suppose so, though if you're worried about your safety, it's a little late for that."

She quickly noted his name: Woodrow Jackson Tanner. His address: RR 4, Tanner Crossing, TX. She looked at the accompanying picture, then glanced at him in surprise, comparing the features. "This picture doesn't look like you at all."

Scowling, he snatched the wallet from her hand. "It's a couple of years old. I've changed."

She cocked her head, amused by his embarrassment. "Actually, I was thinking the picture was quite flattering. You look…friendlier."

He shot her a dark scowl, then jerked a chair from the table and sat down. "Are you going to make coffee, or what?"

"Of course." She headed for the coffeemaker, but stole a glance at him over her shoulder, fearing she'd insulted him with her comment. "I'm sorry if what I said about your photo offended you."

"You had questions," he said tersely.

Reminded of them, she pulled a canister from the cupboard and measured grounds. "Yes. Quite a few, in fact."

"So let's hear 'em."

She switched on the coffeemaker, then crossed to sit opposite him at the table. "Where did Renee live?"

"You don't know?"

"No. I haven't had any contact with my sister in over five years."

Though she sensed that he wanted to quiz her about that, he said instead, "Killeen."

"Killeen," she repeated, amazed to discover that Renee had lived a mere three-hour drive from Dallas. "You said that you didn't know her."

"No. Never even heard of her until Maggie showed up with the kid."

"Which is your father's?"

"Yeah," he muttered, his expression turning sour.

"And he and Renee never married?"

He snorted. "That wasn't his style."

"You sound as if your father was involved in…paternity situations before."

He arched a brow. "More than I was obviously aware of."

She frowned thoughtfully, wondering what Renee would have seen in a man old enough to be her father, then rose to pour them both a cup of coffee. When she returned to the table, she pushed a cup toward him, then closed her hands around hers, needing the warmth.

"How did she die?"

He took a sip. "Something to do with the birth. I don't know the details. Maggie could probably tell you, though."

"Maggie," she repeated. "The friend. You said she's your brother's wife?"

"Yeah. Though that's recent. A couple of days ago, in fact. Ace hired her to take care of the baby, then they up and married."

"They fell in love?" she asked in surprise.

He grimaced at the question. "I guess. If there is such a thing. They seem suited. They're both nuts about the kid. Hell," he said, tossing up a hand. "Come and see for yourself."

Her eyes rounded. "What?"

"Come to Tanner's Crossing with me. See the kid. Meet Ace and Maggie and my other brothers."

The thought of going to Tanner's Crossing and coming face to face with her sister's past terrified her. What kind of person had Renee become? Would the baby look like Renee? Would Elizabeth be able to let her niece go once she saw her, held her in her arms?

She swallowed hard. "I'll need to pack a bag."

Two

—

Woodrow had thought Elizabeth would sleep during the drive to Tanner's Crossing. At least that was the impression she'd given him, when she'd tipped her head back against the seat and closed her eyes as he'd pulled away from her house. But she hadn't slept. He knew, because her facial muscles had remained tense throughout the drive and she'd kept her hands knotted together on her lap so tightly her knuckles gleamed a pearly white in the darkness. He'd considered asking her to take over the wheel, so he could sleep. After twenty-four hours without any, he could use a little shut-eye. But after sizing her up, he'd opted to remain in the driver's seat. The woman was skinnier than a rail and looked as weak as a newborn calf, which made him question her ability to handle a truck the size of his.

When he stopped in front of his log house, she finally gave up the possum act and sat up.

"Are we here?" she asked.

Her voice sounded a bit rusty after three hours without use.

"Yeah," he replied, then clarified, "at my place."

She whipped her head around, her eyes wide in alarm. "But I thought we were going to your brother's home."

He gestured at the windshield and the darkness beyond. "It's not daylight yet. Everyone will still be in bed. I figured we'd catch a couple hours sleep, then head over to the Bar T." Without waiting for a reply, he pushed open his door and hopped to the ground. He stretched his arms above his head to smooth out the kinks the drive had left in his back, then dropped his arms with a weary sigh and rounded the hood.

As he opened her door, he saw that her eyes were riveted on the dark house behind him. "Problem?" he asked.

Her gaze snapped to his. She gulped, then forced a polite smile. "I appreciate your consideration. Really I do. But I'm not the least bit tired. Couldn't we just go to your brother's?"

"And chance waking Ace up before he's gotten a full night's rest?" Shaking his head, he offered her a hand. "Trust me. That's not something you want to do."

She gave the dark house another uneasy look, before accepting his hand. "Why not?" she asked as she climbed down.

The moment her feet touched the ground, he released her and reached into the back to lift out her suitcase. "Because he's meaner than a grizzly if he's awakened before he's ready to rise." He tipped his head toward the house, indicating for her to precede him up the rock walk that led to the front porch. "One time when we were out camping during a roundup, Rory and me woke him up from a dead sleep and 'fore we knew what was happening, he had us between the sights of his shotgun."

She jerked to a stop on the porch, her eyes wide in dismay. "He was going to shoot you?"

He gave her a nudge with the suitcase, urging her on to the door. "Didn't hang around long enough to find out. Me and Rory hightailed it out of there so fast, Ace was spittin' dust for a week."

He pushed the door open, then waited for her to enter before him. "Light switch is on the left," he instructed.

As she fumbled a hand on the rough-hewn wall in search of the switch, Elizabeth wondered what had possessed her to agree to making this trip. At the very least, she should have insisted upon driving her own car. If she had, she could be on her way to a hotel right now, rather than searching for a light switch in a strange man's house and worrying about her safety.

Berating herself for the uncustomary impulsiveness, she found the switch and flipped it on. Light flooded the space, exposing a large room. A stone fireplace stood opposite her, wood stacked ready in a copper tub on its hearth. Before it, a round, braided rag rug was spread, covering a large portion of the heart-of-pine flooring. A small kitchen opened to the left of the fireplace, and a closed door stood at its right. To her surprise, she found his home warm and inviting, which helped ease her fears a bit.

"You can bunk down in here," he said as he crossed to open the closed door. He flipped on the overhead light, then tossed her suitcase onto the massive bed that dominated the small room.

Elizabeth stopped in the doorway and stared, knowing by the personal items scattered about that this was his room. "Where will you sleep?" she asked uneasily.

"On the sofa." He leaned to turn on a lamp beside the bed. "If you're worried about hygiene, the sheets are clean. Changed 'em myself before I left for Dallas yesterday morning."

The intimacy suggested in sleeping in a strange man's bed had her taking a nervous step back. "There's no need for you to give up your bed. I'll sleep on the sofa."

"And have my stepmother rolling in her grave?" He shook his head. "No, ma'am. 'Guests take priority over comfort.' That's what Momma Lee always said."

He whipped back the crazy quilt that covered the bed, then turned for the door. "The bath's through there," he said, flapping a hand over his shoulder to indicate a partially open door behind him. "Fresh towels and wash cloths are in the linen chest beside the shower stall. If you wake up first, the coffee makings are in the kitchen cupboard above the percolator. 'Night,'' he said and closed the door behind him.

Elizabeth stared at the door for a good thirty seconds, before finding her voice. "G-good night.''

Woodrow lay sprawled on the sofa, one arm draped over his eyes and a hand splayed over his belly, the tips of three fingers pushed beneath the waistband of his boxer shorts. Though he usually slept in the raw, since he had a guest in the house, he'd thought it best to leave on his shorts. He wasn't modest, but he figured if the doc woke up first and came in to make coffee and caught him sacked out on the sofa in his birthday suit, she'd probably drop dead from a heart attack.

He heard a scratch on the door and swore under his breath, having forgotten about his dog. With a weary sigh, he rolled to his feet, opened the door a crack, just wide enough for Blue to slip through, then shut it and stretched back out on the sofa. A wet nose bumped his arm, followed by a pitiful whimper.

"Sorry, mutt," he grumbled. "There's not room for both of us up here." He lifted a hand and pointed to the rug in front of the fireplace. "You get the rug."

Blue slunk over to the fireplace and flopped down on the rug. The dog let out a low *woof* to let Woodrow know she didn't like the arrangement, then dropped her head between her paws. Within minutes, both Woodrow and Blue were snoring.

* * *

In the next room, Elizabeth lay beneath the covers, wide-eyed, forcing herself to take long, even breaths. It wasn't fear of the man in the other room that kept her awake.

It was regret.

Renee.

Though tears burned behind her eyes and clogged her throat, she couldn't cry. But, oh God, how she wanted to. She wanted to throw open the floodgates and let loose all the emotions she'd suppressed for so many years. Cry until there were no more tears left to be shed, empty herself of every last drop of grief, unwind every thread of restraint, every layer of composure she'd bound herself with for years in order to survive.

Renee.

Even now she could see her younger sister. The white-blond ringlets Elizabeth had lovingly combed and adorned with ribbons each day before sending her younger sister off to school. The sky blue eyes with the mystical power to light up a room or melt the hardest of hearts. The classically beautiful features that Elizabeth had envied so much.

Oh, Renee, she thought sadly. *Where did I go wrong? What could I have done differently? Why did you keep running away? What were you running away from?*

But the dark room offered up no answers, no insight into the questions that had haunted Elizabeth for years.

Rolling to her side, she gathered the covers to her

chin and squeezed her eyes shut, determined to sleep. Using a technique her therapist had suggested to help with the insomnia she suffered, she imagined herself in a peaceful, stress-free environment. With slow, even strokes, she painted in her mind a field of wild-flowers and a stream shaded by trees, their low-hanging branches dipping into the deep, clear water, like long graceful fingers. She placed herself there, stretched out alongside the stream on a soft bed of crushed grass. Scents wafted beneath her nose. The musky smell of rotted leaves and the sharper, sweeter scent of the crushed flowers she lay upon. The sound of the water bubbling over the rocks and the birds chirping in the trees nearby soothed her frayed nerves, while the breeze riffling through her hair and the re-laxing warmth of the sun on her face melted the ten-sion from her body. She stretched lazily, content—

Stiffening, she flipped open her eyes, jerked from the relaxing scene by a sound. The door opening? she wondered, straining to hear. She listened a moment, wondering if perhaps it was Woodrow. She lifted her head to look toward the door, but saw nothing in the darkness. Telling herself she was imagining things, with a frustrated sigh she dropped her head back to the pillow and closed her eyes. She forced her mind back to the peaceful scene, imagining again the field of wildflowers, the stream tumbling over moss-covered rocks. Gradually the tension eased from her body.

She slept.

* * *

A blood-curdling scream rent the air. Woodrow sat bolt upright at the chilling sound, his heart lodged in his throat. Disoriented for a moment, he blinked once. Blinked again. Then he remembered the doc and vaulted from the sofa.

He threw open the bedroom door and hit the overhead light switch. Squinting his eyes against the sudden glare, he focused his gaze on the bed. The doc sat huddled against the headboard, fully dressed, her knees hugged to her chest, her hands clamped over her face.

Blue lay in her customary spot at the foot of his bed.

"Dang you, Blue," he complained. He caught the dog by the scruff of the neck and hauled the animal to the floor. "Out," he ordered, pointing to the door.

Blue slunk from the room, her tail tucked between her legs.

He turned to the doc. "It was just Blue," he explained, then added, "my dog."

Her shoulders drooped in relief and she lowered her hands. "I thought—"

She stopped midsentence, her eyes rounding. She quickly averted her gaze, her cheeks flaming a bright red.

Woodrow glanced down and swore, having forgotten he was wearing nothing but his drawers. But he wasn't about to apologize. Not when it was her scream that had jerked him from a sound sleep and had him barreling into the bedroom.

"You're lucky I've got on shorts," he grumbled as he turned for the den. "Usually I sleep in the raw."

Elizabeth didn't even attempt to go back to sleep. The dog had scared the life out of her when it had jumped onto the bed, but opening her eyes to find Woodrow standing beside the bed, wearing nothing but...

Gulping, she leapt from the bed and all but ran for the bathroom. After locking the door behind her, she bent over the sink and splashed cold water over her flushed face. She groped blindly for a towel and buried her face in its softness.

But she couldn't block the image of the near-naked Woodrow that seemed engraved behind her lids.

Oh, God, was all she could think, gulping again. He was so...so *male.* The broad shoulders. The wide, muscled chest shadowed by dark hair. Arms rippling with muscle. Wide, strong hands. Long, powerful legs stretching from the hem of the powder-blue boxers.

Usually I sleep in the raw.

She groaned, remembering what he'd said, and pressed the towel tighter against her face, trying not to think about what lay beneath those powder-blue boxers. She was a grown woman, she reminded herself sternly. A doctor, for heaven's sake! It wasn't as if she wasn't familiar with the male anatomy. She'd dealt with dozens of male patients during her medical training and residency. And she and Ted had been intimate for over two years.

She dragged the towel from her face and fisted her

hands in it on the edge of the sink, staring at her flushed face. But the sight of Ted's naked body had never left her feeling as weak-kneed and needy as seeing Woodrow in that same state.

Drawing in a deep breath, she unfurled her fingers from the towel. "It was the shock," she told her reflection. Opening her eyes to find Woodrow standing beside the bed in his underwear had been a shock, nothing more.

Though her knees were still a bit unsteady, she turned away from the sink and went back into the bedroom to collect her suitcase. Since she was awake, she decided she might as well freshen up and prepare for her meeting with Woodrow's family and her niece.

It was obvious she wasn't going to get any more sleep.

Not when she knew that a half-naked Woodrow lay sleeping in the next room.

Woodrow paused at the front door, his hand on the knob. "They're good people," he told the doc, hoping to plead Ace and Maggie's case one last time before introducing his brother and sister-in-law to Elizabeth. "They love that kid like she was their own."

Tightening her fingers on her shoulder bag, she gave him a brisk nod. "I'm sure they are," she replied. "I'm grateful for the care they've given my niece."

Which didn't offer Woodrow a clue as to whether

she intended to sign over to Ace and Maggie whatever claim she might have on the kid.

With a sigh, he opened the door and pushed it wide, gesturing for the doc to precede him into the house. "We're here," he called loudly as he followed her inside.

Ace appeared in the doorway to the study, looking as if he hadn't had a decent night's sleep in a month. His eyes were bloodshot and his jaw shadowed by at least two days' worth of stubble.

He started toward them, a hand extended to Elizabeth. "Ace Tanner," he said by way of greeting, then glanced behind him. "And this," he said, reaching to loop an arm around his wife's waist and draw her forward, "is my wife, Maggie."

The doc shook first Ace's hand, then Maggie's, her expression unchanging, her face a cool mask. "Elizabeth Montgomery. It's nice to meet you both."

Maggie nodded a tight-lipped greeting, but said nothing. Woodrow wondered what was wrong with her. Usually his sister-in-law was friendlier than a pup and talkative as a magpie. But this morning she seemed withdrawn, even resentful.

Ace opened an arm in invitation. "Why don't we move into the den, where we can talk more comfortably."

Elizabeth went first. Maggie followed a slow second. Woodrow fell into line behind his sister-in-law and gave Ace a questioning look as he passed by his brother. Ace lifted a shoulder and mouthed "later," before following Woodrow into the den.

"Maggie baked a batch of cinnamon rolls this morning," Ace offered, "and there's a fresh pot of coffee."

Woodrow dropped down onto the sofa next to the doc and rubbed a hand over his stomach. "You won't hear me turning down any of Maggie's cooking."

Ace turned to Elizabeth. "How about you?"

Placing her purse primly on her lap, she folded her hands over it. "No, thank you," she said politely.

"You sure?" Ace asked. "Maggie makes a mean cinnamon roll."

"I'm quite sure they're delicious, but I don't care for anything, thank you."

Ace lifted a shoulder. "Whatever you say." He started for the door, but Maggie beat him there by a foot.

"I'll make Woodrow a plate," she told Ace and darted from the room before he could stop her.

Stifling a sigh, Ace retraced his steps and sank down on an overstuffed chair opposite the sofa. He forced a smile. "How was the trip from Dallas?"

Woodrow glanced at the doc to see if she was going to respond. When she didn't, he said, "It was fine. We hit Tanner's Crossing before dawn, so we stopped by the house to catch a few Zs before heading over here."

Ace nodded, then seemed at a loss as to what to say to fill the awkward silence that followed.

The doc solved the problem for him.

"I'd like to see my niece, if that's all right with you."

"She's still asleep. I thought we'd visit for awhile until she wakes up."

Woodrow could tell by the way the doc pursed her lips, she didn't want to wait, but she nodded her agreement.

Maggie returned with a tray and set it on the coffee table in front of Woodrow.

"You like your coffee black, right, Woodrow?"

He eyed the plate of cinnamon rolls, his mouth watering in anticipation. "Yeah. And about a dozen of those rolls, if you don't mind."

Maggie filled a cup with coffee, then transferred two rolls to a plate and passed it to him.

Woodrow balanced the plate on his thigh and, ignoring the fork she'd provided, picked up a roll and took a healthy-size bite. Groaning, he closed his eyes. "Damn, Maggie. If you weren't already married, I swear I'd drop down on a knee and propose."

"You propose?" she repeated, then snorted a laugh as she sank down on the chair next to Ace. "I thought you were a confirmed bachelor?"

He gulped a swallow of coffee to wash down the roll, then dragged the back of his hand across his mouth. "I am. But a man would be a fool to let a woman who can cook as good as you get away."

Ace laid a possessive hand on Maggie's leg. "Sorry, bro. She's taken."

Elizabeth cleared her throat, drawing their attention to her.

"Woodrow was unable to tell me how Renee

died." She looked to Maggie, directing the question to her. "He said that you'd know."

"Preeclampsia."

"Toxemia," Elizabeth said thoughtfully, then frowned. "I would think her obstetrician would've caught the signs early enough to take the necessary precautions."

Maggie shrugged, looking uncomfortable. "He might've if Star had seen him regularly. From what her doctor told me, after verifying her pregnancy, Star never returned to his office for her prenatal check-ups."

An infant's cry had all four adults jerking to attention.

Maggie leapt to her feet. "That's Laura. I'll get her."

The doc rose and placed a hand on Maggie's arm, stopping her.

"May I?" she asked, then added, "Please?"

Maggie opened her mouth, as if to deny Elizabeth's request. Then flopped back down on her chair and turned her head away. "The nursery's the third door on the left."

Elizabeth followed the sound of the baby's cries down the hall, silently counting the doors she passed. At the third, she paused to take a deep breath, then twisted open the door and stepped inside.

Sunlight greeted her, spilling from tall windows on either side of a crib placed against the opposite wall. A mobile of colorful farm animals bobbed at the crib's head, set into motion by the infant's fussing. Bumper pads covered in pink-and-white gingham lined the crib's sides, blocking Elizabeth's view of the baby. Though she knew her niece lay only a few feet away, she hung back, frightened to take that first step nearer.

Would the baby look like Renee? she worried. Would she have Renee's blond curly hair? Her mesmerizing blue eyes? Her dainty features? Would she, Elizabeth, be able to bear it, if the infant *did* look like Renee?

As the infant's cries grew stronger, she took a cautious step nearer. Another, and a tiny fist appeared above the bumper pads, batting angrily at the air. Another step and she had a clear view of the baby. Her chest tightened painfully at the sight. My niece, she thought, gulping. She took the last step and closed her hands over the top rail of the crib, looked down.

An angel, was all she could think. Though the infant's face was flushed an angry red and tears streaked her cheeks, Elizabeth was sure she was looking into the face of an angel.

The infant's cries rose higher.

Gulping, Elizabeth forced her fingers from the death grip she had on the rail and reached for the baby. She lifted her carefully, turning for the rocker placed before the window as she drew the infant to her breasts. So tiny, she thought as she sank down, her gaze fixed on the infant's features. So perfect. She stroked a finger beneath the baby's eye, and the infant

stopped crying and blinked up at her. Startling blue
eyes glimmered with crystal tears.

Oh, God, she thought, as emotion rose to close her
throat. *Renee.* She looks just like Renee had as a
baby. The same eyes. The same curly, white-blond
hair. Blinded by her own tears, she caught the baby's
hand and brought it her cheek, held it there. A tear
slipped over her bottom lid and fell to splatter on the
infant's gown, leaving a wet spot to spread on the
delicate pink fabric.

Oh, Renee, she cried silently, as the crack in the
dam opened, releasing a flood of emotion. *Why did
you have to die?*

Ace sat on the edge of his chair, his elbows on his
knees, the heels of his hands dug into his forehead.
Maggie paced in front of the fireplace, one arm
hugged at her waist, nervously worrying a thumbnail
between her teeth.

Reared back on the sofa, Woodrow watched them.
He'd never seen two more uptight people in his life.
But he supposed he understood their concern. Even
shared a bit of it. After all, the doc had been in the
nursery for over ten minutes with the kid.

"Do you want me to go and check on her?" he
asked.

Maggie stopped her pacing. "Oh, Woodrow," she
said, her face crumpling in a mixture of relief and
desperation. "Would you?"

Ace glanced up. "No," he said, shaking his head.
"She's entitled to a little time alone with the kid."

"But she's been back there forever!" Maggie cried. "Laura's bound to be hungry. I'll get a bottle," she said and headed for the door.

Ace bolted from his chair and caught her by the arm. "No, Maggie. Give the woman some time."

She struggled to break free. "But, Ace—"

He caught her by both arms and gave her a firm shake. "Maggie. It's only fair."

She dropped her forehead to his chest. "Oh, Ace," she cried, clinging to him. "Please don't let her take Laura away. Please. Don't let her take her."

"Ah, Maggie." Cupping a hand at the nape of her neck, he rested his chin on the top of her head, his Adam's apple bobbing convulsively. "We're going to do everything we can to keep Laura with us. I promise, we will."

Unable to sit by and watch his brother and sister-in-law suffer a minute longer, Woodrow pushed to his feet. "I'll check on the doc. See if she wants to give the kid a bottle."

Ace looked up. "Thanks, Woodrow," he said gratefully. Murmuring softly to Maggie, he drew her back to the chair and pulled her down onto his lap.

Blowing out a long breath, Woodrow headed down the hall for the nursery. He stopped outside the closed door, unsure if he should knock or just walk in. Undecided, he leaned his ear close to the door and listened. Not hearing a sound, he pressed his ear against the wood but still didn't hear anything. Frowning, he straightened and twisted open the door.

The doc sat in the rocking chair in front of the

window, the baby clutched to her breasts. She had her cheek pressed to the infant's and her eyes squeezed shut.

He took a cautious step inside. "Doc?" he said quietly.

When she didn't respond, he crossed to the rocker and dropped down on a knee in front of her. "Doc?" he said again. "You okay?"

She opened her eyes and the grief, the sadness he saw behind the lenses of her glasses, nearly broke his heart.

"R-Renee," she said and clutched the baby tighter against her chest. "She l-looks just like Re-Renee."

Woodrow was at a loss as to what to say, what to do. "I wouldn't know."

"I—I—" A sob rose, choking her. She dropped her head back and gulped, blinking furiously. "I c-couldn't stop h-her. Sh-she kept running a-away."

He laid a hand on her knee, sure that she was talking about her sister. "I doubt it was your fault."

She dropped her chin to look at the baby and a tear slid down her face. "It-it was my fault. I was s-supposed to take c-are of her. W-watch after her."

The tears fell faster now, a steady stream of misery that Woodrow was helpless to stem. Sobs shook her shoulders, seemed to wrack her entire body. He gave her a knee a reassuring squeeze.

"Come on, Doc," he said, trying his best to calm her down. "Crying so hard like that…you'll make yourself sick."

She hugged the baby tighter, rocking slowly back and forth, sobbing uncontrollably.

"Woodrow?"

He glanced behind him and saw Ace standing in the doorway. Maggie stood behind him, straining to see over his shoulder. Both of their faces were creased in concern.

Scowling, he stood. "Here," he said quietly to the doc and reached for the baby. "Let me take her." He quickly carried the infant to Ace and handed her over. "The doc's upset," he said, stating the obvious. "I'll take her home with me and see if I calm her down."

Ace cast a worried look at the doc. "Are you sure you can handle this?"

Woodrow flattened his lips in a grim line. "Doesn't look like I have much choice."

He waited until Maggie and Ace left, then turned back to the doc. She sat in the rocker, bent at the waist, sobbing, her shoulders shaking hard enough to crack bone. Puffing his cheeks, he let out a breath, then crossed to drop to a knee in front of her again.

"Doc?" he said quietly. "Let's you and me go back to my place. Give you a chance to pull yourself together."

When she only cried harder, he dragged a handkerchief from his back pocket and pressed it into her hand.

She fisted it beneath her nose. "Th-they must think I'm c-crazy."

"Ace and Maggie?" Shaking his head, he reached up and slipped off her glasses, tucked them into his shirt pocket. "Don't you worry about them," he assured her as he rose. "They understand. Now dry your eyes and I'll take you back to my place."

She shook her head frantically, tears streaming down her face. "I—I c-can't s-stop crying."

"Then don't." He bent and hefted her up into his arms. "Something tells me you're long overdue."

By the time Woodrow made the drive back to his house, the doc was asleep, obviously having worn herself out from all the crying. Rather than wake her and take a chance on her falling apart again, he bundled her up into his arms and carried her inside. As he laid her down on the bed, she clung to him.

"Don't leave," she begged pitifully. "Please."

Woodrow wasn't a man long on patience and he sure as hell had no use for crybabies, but he figured holding her awhile longer was a sight less bothersome than dealing with another crying jag should she start bawling again. Resigned to the chore, he stretched out on the bed beside her and held her.

Though she immediately dropped off to sleep again, her head pillowed in the crook of his arm, her body half draped over his, convulsions continued to wrack her slim body, aftereffects of the long crying jag, he was sure.

She wasn't any bigger than a minute and weaker than a newborn pup, he thought, reminded again of her petiteness. He craned his neck to peer down at her face. The tears had washed off most of what little makeup she wore, exposing dark circles beneath her eyes. Problem sleeping? he wondered and shifted his gaze to the hand she held against his chest. The nails were bitten back to the quick.

Pensive, he laid his head back, remembering the pink splotches he'd noticed on her neck when he'd first seen her at her office. He wondered if they were a result of her emotional state rather than a rash or a birthmark, as he'd originally assumed.

The woman was a basket case, he decided. Granted, the last eighteen hours had been tough on her. Within a short period of time, she'd learned of her sister's death, then traveled through the night to see a niece she hadn't known existed. But something told him that neither of those things was the cause of her current state.

During the crying jag, she'd said something about her sister running away and it being all her fault. But all that had to have happened years ago, he thought, frowning. The doc, herself, had told him that she hadn't seen her sister in over five years.

If that was the case, then why did the doc blame herself for her sister's death? And how did her relationship with her sister figure into the nervous rash and the bitten-down nails?

Three

Woodrow returned to the cabin at dusk in his usual manner. Loudly. After scraping the mud and muck from his boots on the grate at the base of the front porch steps, he whistled up Blue and clomped inside with the dog close on his heels. It wasn't until he had slammed the door behind him that he remembered the doc. Swearing under his breath, he crossed to the bedroom door to see if he'd awakened her. He found her still curled on his bed asleep, the quilt he'd tossed over her before leaving to check on his livestock seemingly undisturbed.

Just seeing her lying there was enough to make his head ache again. How in the hell had he gotten stuck with her, anyway? he asked himself.

He turned away, with a scowl. Because he was a

sucker. That's why. He wanted to blame Ace for his being saddled with her. But he was honest enough to admit that it wasn't Ace's fault the doc was in his bed. She wasn't the first stray he'd dragged home. Over the years he'd taken in more injured and abandoned animals than he cared to count. After regaining their strength, some had left of their own accord. Others he'd found homes for. A few, like Blue, had decided to hang their hats alongside his and had stayed.

He wondered what the doc would do.

Snorting a breath, he dropped down on the sofa and toed off his boots. Hell, the doc wasn't some abandoned puppy in need of a few square meals and a warm rug in front of the fire. She was a human being. A woman. She wasn't staying. Hell, he didn't want her to! She'd sleep off the exhaustion the crying jag had left her with, decide what she wanted to do about the kid, then head back to Dallas and that big-ass house of hers planted in that fancy-dancy neighborhood with the houses shoved up so close to each other, when one homeowner sneezed, the whole block caught a cold.

Ripping open the snaps of his chambray shirt, he flopped back against the sofa to glare at the open bedroom door and the shadowed S-shape her curled body created beneath the quilt. She was a case. No doubt about it. Nothing but a bundle of wired nerves on the verge of shorting out...

He narrowed his eyes thoughtfully. Or maybe she'd already shorted out. He'd never seen a person cry so hard or for so long a period of time. He wouldn't soon forget the desperate way she'd clung to him, the heartbreaking plea in her voice when she'd begged him to stay after he'd laid her down on the bed. He rubbed a hand over his heart and the dull ache that throbbed to life there. It had been a long time since anyone had needed him. Longer still since he'd felt inclined to respond to a need.

As he continued to stare, she shifted and the quilt he'd draped over her slipped, exposing a slim hip, reminding him of the feel of her body nestled against his as he'd lain beside her. The softness. The fragility. He hadn't shared a bed with a woman in a long time, experienced the warmth of having a body other than Blue's curled against his. It was a pleasant feeling, one that, even now, made his groin tighten with need.

Setting his jaw against the attraction, he forced his gaze away. He was tired, he told himself. Physically and mentally exhausted. Otherwise, he wouldn't be thinking sexual thoughts about the doc. What he needed was sleep. About twenty-fours of it. He glanced down the length of the sofa and stifled a groan, knowing it lacked about a foot in accommodating his long frame and about a mile in comfort. He sure as hell wouldn't be getting much rest if he slept here. He looked back at the bedroom door and his bed. It was big, he told himself. Plenty big enough for two to sleep on without one disturbing or possibly even being aware of the other. Chances were, he'd wake up before she did anyway.

Decided, he peeled off his shirt and rose, dropping the shirt on the floor behind him as he headed for his

room. At the side of the bed, he flipped back his belt
buckle and unhooked his jeans, then eased down on
the side of the mattress, shoved his pants to his an-
kles, kicked them off. He hooked his thumbs in the
waistband of his boxers, intending to shed them, too,
then thought better of it. No need in upsetting the doc
further, if she happened to wake up first. Having her
discover that he'd crawled into bed with her was one
thing. Having her discover that he'd done so buck-
naked was asking for trouble.

Sighing, he lay back, slung an arm over his eyes.
Two breaths later, he was asleep.

Elizabeth slept for over eighteen hours straight. She
didn't dream. An oddity for her. Usually her sleep
was filled with dreams, mostly of the nightmare va-
riety, which was one of the main causes of the insomnia she suffered. When she did stir, she felt as if she
was coming out from under an anesthetic: her limbs
leaden, her eyelids too heavy to open. Though she
struggled toward wakefulness, the seductive darkness
pulled at her, drawing her back. As she drifted toward
unconsciousness again, she imagined herself a co-
coon, totally surrounded. Padded. Protected. Or perhaps she was a spoon. The shape was right. She could
see herself neatly tucked inside a felt-lined drawer,
with another spoon aligned directly behind her. But
what was the weight that held her down, the one that
seemed centered in the curve of her waist?

As her sleep-drugged mind pondered this complex-
ity, she shifted, settling her hips more comfortably

into the bowl shape behind her. At the movement, she heard a low moan, felt a warm rush of air at her ear. And pressure, she realized, startled by it. Focusing on the pressure, she became aware of the hand splayed across her stomach, the fingers that drew her hips more firmly into the curve of the bowl. The warmth of each blunt-tipped finger burned into her skin, awakening her mind, arousing her senses.

Woodrow.

Even as his name formed in her mind, she knew this was no felt-lined drawer she lay upon. It was a bed. Woodrow's bed. And it was Woodrow behind her, not a spoon. She opened her eyes to stare at the shadowed wall opposite her, every nerve ending in her body alive and thrumming. Woodrow was in bed with her, holding her? But…why?

The why wasn't important, she told herself, and closed her eyes with a contented sigh. Not when she could savor the pleasant sensation of simply being held. She concentrated on the peace and comfort his presence provided, anxious to draw as much from the experience as she could. But her awareness of the man quickly grew, distracting her. The strength in the arm curled around her; the muscled wall of the chest pressed against her back.

He wasn't wearing a shirt, she realized with a suddenness that had her breath catching in her throat. She pushed a tentative foot along the length of his leg. Nor any pants. Her heart kicked into a faster beat. Was he nude? He'd told her he usually slept in the raw. Anxious to discover whether he was dressed or not, she moved her hips against his groin. The soft rasp of cotton against her linen slacks confirmed that he was at least partially dressed. She wasn't sure if she was disappointed or relieved to discover that he'd maintained at least that modicum of modesty.

Why was he holding her? she wondered, her mind drifting back to her original thought. And how long had been doing so? She vaguely recalled asking him to stay with her when he'd first laid her down. She glanced at the window beside the bed and was surprised to see that it was dark outside. Had she slept away the day? she wondered in confusion.

She tried to sit up, in order to see the clock on the bedside table, but the fingers resting against her belly tightened, holding her in place.

"Stay," he murmured sleepily. "Feels good."

Eyes wide, her heart in her throat, she sank back down, resting her head on the pillow in front of his again. He shifted her hips back into the masculine curve of his and sighed, seemingly satisfied with their positions. She could feel the moist warmth of his breath on her neck, the even rise and fall of his chest against her back, and knew he slept.

The idea that he was behind her, sharing the same bed with her, kept her eyes wide and her mind racing. Had he been there all day? As hard as she tried, she couldn't remember anything beyond the moment he'd laid her on his bed.

No, she thought, gulping. She did remember some things. She remembered the slow drag of his hand up and down her back as he'd soothed her. The solace she'd found in the sound of his low, husky voice as he'd murmured quietly to her. The comfort she'd found in his arms.

He was so big. So gruff. Yet, he'd treated her with a gentleness, a tenderness that defied his bearlike appearance, his grouchy demeanor.

Confused by the paradox he presented, she focused her mind on the memory of his caress. He has wonderful hands, she thought. Wide. Sure. Even with his fingers lax against her stomach, as they were now, she sensed the strength within them. And his eyes, she thought. She closed her own, picturing the blue in his. The first time she'd seen him, she remembered thinking his eyes had seemed harsh. Even cold. But when he'd knelt before the rocker and drawn off her glasses, she'd detected a softness in them, a tenderness that defied that first impression.

So which was he? she asked herself, her confusion returning. Gruff or tender? And why was he being so kind to her? He didn't know her. Had no ties or obligations to her.

Even as the questions formed in her mind, she became aware of the increased pressure of his fingers on her stomach, pulling her back, the slow roll of his groin against her hips. She recognized the subtle swell of his erection and heat flooded her, turning her body molten.

Twenty-four hours before, if she'd awakened and found herself in bed with a stranger—an *aroused* stranger—she would have bolted from the bed in fear. But for some odd reason, she wasn't afraid. Not of

Woodrow. At the moment, she felt nothing but…
contentment? Most assuredly. Pleasure? Yes, that,
too. Lust? Shivering deliciously, she snuggled closer
to him. Oh, yes. Definitely lust.

Hugging the sheet to her chin, she closed her
eyes…and slept.

When Elizabeth awakened again, sunshine spilled
through the window beside the bed. Missing the
warmth that had enveloped her through the night, she
dropped a hand behind her, expecting to find Woodrow behind her, but the sheets were cool to her touch.
Had she been dreaming? she asked herself in confusion.

"Over here."

Jerking up to an elbow, she looked over her shoulder and found Woodrow reared back in a chair beside
the door, watching her, a steaming mug of coffee balanced on his belt buckle, a finger hooked loosely in
its thick handle.

Rolling to her hips, she braced herself up with her
hands to stare at him. "You did sleep with me," she
whispered in disbelief.

He snorted a laugh. "Not in the biblical sense, if
that's what you're worried about."

She pressed a hand to her forehead and sat up,
shaking her head. "No, no. I thought you were
a…dream."

He dropped the chair to all four legs and stood.
"Better a dream than a nightmare."

She lifted her face, keeping her gaze on his as he

rose. As she continued to stare, memories of the previous day's events flooded her mind. Her emotional collapse upon seeing and holding her niece. Woodrow carrying her to his truck and driving her back to his cabin. Lying with him, nestled against his chest. Waking hours later to find him in bed with her, asleep, his arms wrapped around her.

Heat flooded her cheeks as she remembered the slow, mesmerizing stroke of his fingers over her stomach, the swell of his arousal against her buttocks. Did he remember that, as well? she wondered. Had he really been asleep? Or had he been awake and aware of her response to him?

Fearing that he would notice the rush of color to her face, she pressed a hand against her cheek. "I—I'm sorry I fell apart at Ace's. You must all think I'm crazy."

He gulped a drink of coffee, then shook his head. "No apology necessary. You were due a good cry. Hungry?" he asked. "I made pancakes. They're probably still warm."

She swung her legs off the bed and headed for the adjoining bath, grateful that he seemed unaware of the night's events. "Famished. I feel as if I haven't eaten in days."

"Judging by your size, I'd say months."

She paused, a hand on the door, and glanced back, expecting to find disgust in his gaze or, at the very least disapproval. But what she found was... What? she wondered.

Before she could name the emotion she found in his eyes, he turned away.

"Be quick," he called over his shoulder. "Those pancakes are getting colder by the minute."

After breakfast, Elizabeth insisted upon cleaning up the kitchen, claiming it was the least she could do, since Woodrow had cooked their meal. Though he was accustomed to doing for himself, he let her, thinking the activity would take her mind off her troubles.

She looked none the worse for wear, he decided, as he watched her from his place at the table. Considering all she'd been through over the last forty-eight hours, she looked pretty damn good. Before joining him in the kitchen for breakfast, she'd combed her hair back into the neat little bun she wore it in and changed into a fresh set of clothes—beige linen slacks and a crisp, white, long-sleeved blouse she wore with the tail out. She still looked fragile enough to break at the slightest jostling, but the sleep must have helped, because the dark circles beneath her eyes had faded somewhat and her cheeks seemed to have a little more color in them.

City life, he thought, with a rueful shake of his head, convinced that it was her life in the city that was responsible for at least part of her weakened state. Shoved up tight against a mass of crawling humanity and breathing nothing but polluted air all day... What the woman needed was a month of good country living, where there was plenty of sunshine and clean, fresh air for the taking.

He rolled his eyes at his own foolishness. How the doc chose to live her life was none of his business. His job had been, first, to find her, then persuade her to give up her rights to her niece, so Ace and Maggie could adopt the kid. He'd accomplished the finding part and now it was time to get busy on the second.

With that in mind, he said, "Think you're up to going over to Ace and Maggie's this morning?"

She stiffened at the question, then forced her shoulders to relax and sank her hands into the dishwater to pull the plug.

"No," she said, shaking her head as she drew her hands from the water. "Not yet." She reached for the dish towel, drying her hands as she turned to face him. "But I would like to visit my sister's grave. Do you know where she's buried?"

Caught off guard by her request, it took a moment for him to respond. "No. But I can find out. Maggie'll know."

At the mention of Maggie, she dropped her gaze, twisting the towel around the fingers of one hand. "She doesn't like me."

"Maggie?" he asked, though he knew exactly who she was talking about and why she might think his sister-in-law disliked her. "Maggie's good as gold and has a heart as big as Texas. It's not that she doesn't like you. It's just that...well, I imagine she's feeling a bit threatened right now."

She glanced up, her forehead pleating. "By me? Why?"

Unsure how to handle this, how much to say, Woodrow blew out a breath, then pushed back his chair and stood, deciding honesty was probably best. "She's afraid you're going to fight her and Ace for custody of the kid." He waited a beat, then asked hesitantly, "Are you?"

She stared at him a moment, then turned away, carefully folding the towel and laying it on the counter beside the sink. "I don't know," she said, her voice trembling a bit. "This has all been so sudden. So unexpected. I lost my sister and now I'm expected to decide the future of my niece." Dipping her chin, she shook her head. "I can't do that until I've dealt with my sister's death." She turned to look at him, her gaze pleading with him to understand. "I know that probably sounds evasive, or at the very least, self-serving, but—" She lifted a hand, then let it drop helplessly to her side, her eyes filling with tears. "I never even got to say goodbye."

Woodrow pulled his truck to a stop on the narrow, tree-lined lane alongside a long row of low tombstones, then stole a glance at the doc, wondering if she was up to this. She'd made the drive to Killeen in silence, and now sat with her face turned to the passenger window, looking out at the cemetery, making it impossible for him to gauge her emotions, her thoughts.

Stifling a sigh, he pointed toward a mound of dirt

with a steel placard marking the grave. "That should be it," he said. "Lot No. 49."

She drew in a long breath, nodded.

"Do you want me to go with you?" he asked.

She shook her head and reached for the door handle. "No. I'll be okay."

He watched her slide down from the cab and walk toward the grave, her steps slow, almost reluctant. A light breeze teased tendrils of hair from her bun and blew them across her face. Reaching up to hold them back, she stopped in front of the grave, and looked down. Woodrow watched, his breath burning a hole in his lungs. After what seemed like a lifetime, she sank to knees, her descent as slow and graceful as that of a leaf falling from a tree. Reaching out a tentative hand, she touched a finger to the plastic shield that protected the card identifying the grave as that of her sister. She stared, gently stroking her finger over the typed words.

Should he go to her? he wondered. Or should he honor her right to privacy and remain in the truck? While he squirmed on the seat, trying to decide what to do, he saw her chin dip to her chest, her shoulders hitch. Swearing under his breath, he shoved open his door.

He reached her in five steps and hunkered down behind her, placing a hand on her shoulder. He didn't say anything. Didn't have the words he felt she needed to ease her grief. Wishing like hell he did, he squeezed her shoulder, silently willing to her what he had to give. His strength.

After a moment, she drew in a deep, shuddery breath and lifted her head, turning her face up to the sky.

"God, I hate this," she said, in a voice thick with tears. "I've dealt with death hundreds of times over the years. As a doctor, even fought it a few times and won." She looked down at the grave and shook her head. "But I'll never understand it. Never."

He gave her a shoulder a reassuring squeeze. "I don't know anybody who does."

She reached up and covered his hand with hers. "It doesn't seem fair, does it?" she asked quietly, her gaze on the grave. "She was so young. A new mother. She had her whole life ahead of her."

"No," he agreed. "It doesn't seem fair. But life rarely does."

She glanced back at him, the tears that still clung to her lashes glimmering like diamonds in the sunshine.

"Have you ever lost anyone close to you, Woodrow?"

He didn't want to go there. Wouldn't. He'd spent the better part of his life steeling his heart against the pain of losing. Frowning, he caught her fingers in his and stood, drawing her to her feet, as well. "It's hard to go through life and not lose someone."

She turned to look at the grave again, her shoulders drooping. "I've lost everyone. My father when I was a child. Mother five years ago. Renee came home for her funeral. That was the last time I ever saw her."

"Did y'all have words?" he asked, then shook his head. "Sorry. That's none of my business."

She glanced back and smiled softly. "It's okay. And, yes, we had words. It seemed, whenever we were in the same room for more than five minutes, we ended up arguing."

She looked beyond him, as if at a distant memory. "We were different. In personality. Looks. We wanted different things out of life. I was always studious. Focused. I knew from the time that I was a little girl that I wanted to be a doctor. Renee wanted..."

When she hesitated, he asked, "What?"

She shifted her gaze back to his, then smiled sadly and shook her head. "I don't know. Everything, I guess. Renee was beautiful and...spoiled." Drawing her hand from his, she dropped her gaze, as if feeling badly for speaking ill of her sister. "I know that probably sounds mean, even cruel, considering she's... gone. But it's the truth." She looked up at him, her eyes brimming with fresh tears. "The sad part is, I helped spoil her."

Woodrow didn't want to feel sorry for her. Didn't want to feel anything for the doc at all. Doing so might jeopardize his ability to persuade her to turn over custody of the kid to Ace and Maggie. But he couldn't just stand by and watch her beat herself up for events that were obviously out of her control. What she needed was a distraction. And he knew the perfect activity to take her mind off her troubles.

"Have you ever been fishing?"

She blinked, confused by the sudden change in topic. "What?"

"Fishing," he repeated. He slung an arm over her shoulders and headed her back to the truck. "I've got a hankerin' for a mess of fried catfish, and I know just this spot where we can catch us a few."

Her nose wrinkled in distaste, Elizabeth contemplated the open carton of chicken hearts sitting on the dock between her and Woodrow. She'd never fished in her life and didn't particularly care about learning how now. But she hadn't wanted to refuse Woodrow's invitation. Not after all he'd done for her.

Determined to be a good sport, she unbuttoned the cuffs of her blouse and neatly folded her sleeves back to her elbows. She eyed the slimy bait, her stomach turning squeamish. She swallowed back the nausea. "Is it really necessary to put one of these on the hook?"

His attention focused on his fishing line, Woodrow spared her a glance. "It is if you want to catch a fish." He turned his gaze back to his line. "And remember to weave it through the hook a couple of times like I showed you. Otherwise it'll fall off when you cast your line."

Closing her eyes, she dipped her hand into the carton, then yanked it back to clutch against her middle. "I can't," she wailed miserably.

He glanced over and frowned at the sick look on her face. Shaking his head, he wedged his fishing rod between his propped up knees and reached for her hook. "Sissy," he muttered.

She turned her face away, unable to watch him bait the hook.

"There," he said, after finishing the task. "Do I need to cast for you, too?"

Determined to prove that she wasn't a sissy, she drew the rod back over her shoulder. "No, I can handle it from here." She pressed her thumb against the reel release as he'd shown her earlier, then slung her arm forward and watched in wide-eyed wonder as the baited hook sailed through the air.

"Set your reel!"

She jumped at the shouted order, murmured a flustered, "Oh, right," and quickly cranked the wheel, until she heard the reel click into place, locking the line. The hook sank out of sight, leaving the red-and-white plastic cork Woodrow had attached to her line to bob on the water's smooth surface, marking its location.

"Now what?" she asked, releasing the breath she'd been holding.

"Now you wait."

Resigned to the task, she folded her legs in front of her, rested the rod in between them and waited. She quickly grew bored with watching the bobbing cork's slow movements and let her gaze stray to her surroundings.

The lake he had brought her to was large, covering ten acres, she remembered him saying, and was framed on two sides by jagged walls of rock. Cedar trees grew from crevices carved into the wall by nature, as did tufts of native grass. Cattle and goats grazed in the pastures that surrounded them.

"Is all of this yours?" she asked curiously.

"What?"

"This," she said, spreading an arm to encompass the land surrounding them.

"Seven hundred and fifty acres of it is." He lifted a hand and pointed in the far distance. "See that gate over there? Just at the top of that rise."

She squinted her eyes behind her sunglasses to better see. "Yes."

"That line of fence is the north boundary." He looked over his shoulder. "You can't see the south boundary for the trees, but it's about the same distance from here as the north. The highway we came in on marks the east, and the west is about a mile and a half that way," he said, pointing. "My cabin sits dead center."

She looked around, marveling at the fact that there wasn't another house in sight. "Don't you get lonely out here?"

His gaze on his cork, he shook his head. "Nope."

She considered that for a moment. "Well, I guess if you did, you could always drive over to your brother's house and visit with him."

He glanced over his shoulder at her. "Ace?" At her nod, he snorted and turned his gaze back to the lake. "Ace doesn't live there. That's the home place. He's only staying there until the old man's estate is settled. His home is in Kerrville."

Surprised to learn that, she said, "You mentioned that you have other brothers. Do they live nearby?"

"Nope. Ry lives in Austin. He's a surgeon. Rory, he's the youngest, he stays in the middle of the road most of the time, chasing between the western stores he owns around the state, but he calls San Antonio home. Whit, he's my stepbrother, lives the closest, about twenty miles from here, but I rarely see him."

"Why not?"

He shrugged. "He has his life. I have mine."

"Your other brothers…are you close to any of them?"

"At one time." Frowning, he focused his gaze on his cork. "Are you going to fish or talk?"

Which meant he didn't want to answer any more of her questions. Honoring his wishes, she patted a hand at the perspiration that misted her neck and shifted her gaze to the live oak and post oak trees that shaded the bank to her right.

That shade looks awfully inviting, she thought wistfully. The weather was unseasonably hot for September, plus she was unused to being outside during the heat of the day. She glanced toward Woodrow, wondering if he was bothered by the heat or if he was accustomed to it.

She was sitting far enough behind him that she could study him without him being aware of her scrutiny. A cowboy hat shaded his face and neck. She stifled a sigh, wishing he had offered her a hat to wear. Her skin was fair and she knew from experience that she'd burn if she stayed out in the sun much longer.

He wasn't totally immune to the heat, though, she thought with a smidgen of satisfaction. A damp stripe of perspiration ran down the middle of his back, an indication that he was perspiring as much as she. She followed the stripe until it disappeared into the waist of his jeans and swallowed hard as her gaze settled on his rear end. He's very well built, she thought, finding it impossible to look away. His body formed a natural V from his shoulders to his hips. She remembered hearing her receptionist, who was a big George Strait fan, refer to the country western singer as having a "cowboy butt." In Elizabeth's estimation, Woodrow's butt put George's to shame.

"You've got a bite."

Startled from her lustful thoughts, she snapped her gaze to the back of Woodrow's head. "What?"

He pointed at her cork. "You've got a bite."

She glanced toward the spot where her cork bobbed in time to see it disappear. Feeling the accompanying tug on her rod, she gasped and scrambled to her feet. "What do I do?" she cried, panicking.

He set his rod aside and scooted out of her way, giving her room. "Reel him in."

She wound frantically, sure that by the tension the fish was placing on her rod, she'd caught a whale. The fish broke through the water, flipped, then dove beneath the surface again. She cranked until the cork bumped the end of her rod, then moved to the edge of the dock, to look down. "It's big, isn't it?" she said, awed by the blurred sight of the fish beneath the water.

"Big enough." He leaned over the dock and caught her line, pulling it up for her to see the catfish that dangled from its end. "Three pounds, if it's an ounce," he told her proudly.

She watched in wide-eyed fascination as he pried the hook from the fish's mouth, then attached the fish to a stringer tied to the dock's post. He leaned over, dropping the stringer back into the water. Sitting back, he wiped his hands down his thighs and shot her a wink. "Good job."

Elizabeth flushed at his praise. It was silly, she knew, but winning his approval meant more to her than any of the awards or degrees she'd earned over the years.

Four

While Elizabeth showered and changed, Woodrow took advantage of her absence to check in with Ace. He stepped outside to make the call, using his cell phone, in order to assure his privacy.

"Yeah," he replied to Ace's question. "I took her to the cemetery." He dropped down on the side of the porch beside Blue and laid a hand on his dog's head. "She handled it okay," he said as he scratched the mutt's ears, then added wryly, "She didn't fall apart like she did yesterday at your house."

"You've been at the cemetery all day?" Ace asked in surprise.

Woodrow shook his head. "No. We left there about noon. After we got back to my place, I took her fishing."

"Fishing?" Ace repeated, laughing. "Hard to imagine the prim and proper doctor doing any serious fishing."

A smile chipped at the corner of Woodrow's mouth as he pictured the doc standing on the pier in her linen slacks and crisp, white blouse, the sleeves shoved up to her elbows, her hair twisted up in that fussy little bun she liked to wear it in, reeling in that catfish. "She's not ready for any tournaments," Woodrow replied, "but she did all right. Caught the biggest fish."

"She outfished *you?*" Ace whooped a laugh.

Woodrow scowled. "I didn't say she outfished me, only that she caught the biggest one."

"Oh. Right," Ace replied, but Woodrow heard the amusement in his brother's voice.

With his manly pride in danger of suffering a mortal blow, Woodrow directed the conversation back to the purpose of his call. "I don't know when she's going to want to see the kid again. She hasn't said any more about it. Maybe tomorrow. I'll let you know."

"What are you going to do with her in the meantime?"

"What do you mean, *do with her?*"

"You know. Entertain her. I can't see the two of you sitting around your cabin, drinking beer and shooting the bull. The doc strikes me as the wine and Socrates type. An intellectual."

Woodrow bristled. "And you think I'm too dumb

to carry on a conversation with an intelligent woman.''

''Now wait a minute, Woodrow. I didn't mean that the way it—''

''Forget it,'' Woodrow grumbled, knowing that the jab at his intellectual prowess—intended or not—was probably deserved. Woodrow had never been a very good student. Had never cared enough to try. Had never had a parent around who'd cared enough to *make* him try.

''I'll call you when she's ready to see the kid again,'' he muttered, then broke the connection.

Tossing the phone down, he braced his forearms on his knees and scowled out at his land. He might not have a college degree like his brothers, he thought defensively. But, by God, he was no dummy. He'd worked hard, saved his money and bought this place, without help from anyone, least of all, his old man. Using what brains he had—plus a hell of lot of sweat and muscle—he'd turned the place into a profitable ranch. Nothing like the Bar T. Granted. But he was proud of what he'd accomplished, what he'd built.

He ran a good-size herd of cattle and goats, cut and sold hay from fields he'd cleared and planted himself. And he'd been studying up on catfish farming, thinking a little diversification might be wise, in the event the bottom fell out of the cattle and goat markets.

He depended on no one, not even nature, for his existence. Though he could easily have tied into the local water district's system when he'd built his cabin, he'd dug a well for his personal use and harvested rainwater from the roofs of his cabin and barns to water his stock and gardens. He'd taken the easy route for his power, signing on with the rural electric co-operative and running electrical lines from the poles at the main road to his house. But he had his own solar generator should the electricity ever fail. And he provided most of the food that he put on his table. The vegetables and fruits he ate came from his own gardens, and his meat from beef he raised and butchered himself.

No, he might not be an intellectual, as Ace had unwittingly reminded him. But he was no dummy. He knew how to survive.

He'd been doing it for years.

Alone.

He heard the hinges on the screen door squeak behind him and glanced over his shoulder just as Elizabeth stepped out onto the porch. Fresh from her shower, she wore an ankle-length, shapeless dress, made out of some gauzy-looking fabric and her feet were bare. Oblivious to his presence, she bent at the waist, letting her hair fall over her face. He watched her drag a brush from the nape of her neck down to the curled ends that curtained her face. He couldn't say what it was he found so erotic about watching such a simple task, but his mouth dried up faster than a pond after a seven-year drought and his jeans shrunk in width a full size.

With her stooped over as she was, her dress gaped at the neckline, providing Woodrow with a limited but interesting view of her breasts. Small, firm mounds, round and full enough to create a narrow valley between, gleamed before his eyes like polished, porcelain globes. His view ended where a sliver of darker flesh, a dusty pink in color, curved beneath the gauzy fabric and disappeared from sight, hiding her nipples from him.

As he watched, she straightened and tossed back her hair. It tumbled around her shoulders, a silken waterfall of shimmering burnished gold in the fading sunlight. With a contented sigh, she turned and her gaze struck his. She tensed, her fingers convulsing on the brush's wooden handle.

"If you'd rather be alone," she said quickly, "I can go back inside."

Woodrow wondered what it was in his expression that would made her think such a thing. Frowning, he shook his head and turned to look out at his land again. "I wasn't doing anything but enjoying the view. There's plenty enough for two."

He heard the soft pad of her feet on the wooden planks of the porch behind him and dropped his hands between his knees to hide his arousal. As she sank down beside him, the hem of her dress brushed his thigh, an unintentional caress that had him swallowing a groan.

Her gaze on the horizon, she pulled her knees up and tucked her dress's hem over her bare feet. A soft smile curved her lips. "It's beautiful."

He followed the line of her gaze to the sunset. "Yeah," he agreed. "It is that."

"It sounds ridiculous, I know, but we don't see

sunsets like this in the city. At least, not where I live.''

He nodded, understanding what she meant. ''Cities have too many buildings for a person to see much of anything. And all those lights?'' He shook his head and gestured toward the reds, pinks and golds embla-zoned on the horizon. ''The illumination from 'em diminishes the sunset's colors. Makes 'em looked all washed out.''

She tilted her head, as if considering his explana-tion. ''I never thought of it that way before,'' she said thoughtfully, then glanced over at him and smiled. ''But you're right. The colors are bolder here, more vibrant.''

He knew that she had spoken, but couldn't have repeated her words if somebody had put a gun to his head and demanded he do so. The moment she'd smiled, it was if something had wrapped itself around his chest and squeezed, her smile's effect on him was that strong. It transformed her face, illuminated her eyes.

Her eyes, he thought, noticing for the first time how beautiful they were. Why hadn't he noticed them be-fore? Maybe because, tonight, she wasn't wearing her glasses. Without the distracting frames and lenses, he saw that her eyes were almond-shaped and framed by long, thick lashes. Though blue like his, the irises in hers were shades lighter, making them appear softer. Kinder. Looking into them was like peering into a deep pool that reflected her soul. Every emotion she felt was there for him to see, every shadow on her heart exposed.

As he stared, tongue-tied by the beauty of her eyes and the secrets they held, a cloud of uncertainty swept over them. She lifted a hand to her cheek. "Do I have something on my face?"

He shook his head, but it took a moment for him to find his voice. "No. There's nothing wrong with your face." When she continued to hold her hand there self-consciously, he caught it and drew it down. "Your face is perfect. I promise."

Her blush was the shade of innocence and touched his heart in a way nothing had in a long time. He should have released her hand then. Instead, he found himself lacing his fingers through hers and drawing it to rest with his on his thigh. She didn't attempt to pull away, but he felt the tremble of her fingers within his and wondered at it.

She was a mature woman. Having a man hold her hand shouldn't spook her. Was it *him* who made her uneasy? he wondered. Or was her uneasiness due to something else?

Like a man back in Dallas.

He swore silently, not having considered the possibility.

He curled his fingers tighter around hers, determined to find out. "Doc, I know there's probably a more delicate way of asking this, but damned if I know what it is." He inhaled a bracing breath, then asked in a rush, "Has someone staked a claim on you?"

She blinked at him in confusion. "What?"

"Do you have a boyfriend?" he asked impatiently.

He detected a flicker of something in her eyes, before she looked away. Something that looked suspiciously like guilt.

"I did," she said quietly, then sighed and turned back to meet his gaze. "But not any longer."

Relief washed through him waves. Pushing off the porch, he stood and drew her up to stand opposite him. "Good. Because I sure wouldn't want someone to come gunning for me."

She sputtered a laugh. "Why would anyone come—"

Before she could finish the question, he slipped his arms around her waist and pulled her hips to his. As he lowered his face over hers, he saw the surprise that flared in her eyes, a split second before he touched his lips to hers.

He didn't thrust his tongue down her throat or rip off her dress...though he had a powerful urge to do both. Instead, he kept the kiss light, the pressure of his mouth on hers nonthreatening. It was the right thing to do. He knew it the moment he felt the soft melting of her body against his, the slow parting of her lips beneath his. Only then did he dare deepen the kiss.

She tasted so sweet, so innocent. Felt so incredibly *right* in his arms. Soft. Utterly feminine...and totally naked beneath the gauzy dress. He first suspected this when her breasts flattened beneath his chest's urging. He knew it for a fact when his hands encountered no bra straps or elastic panty bands on their downward path to her hips.

Cupping her low, he lifted her, holding her against him, and groaned as the hard ridge of her pelvic bone grazed his arousal.

His blood pumped hot through his veins, his pulse roared in his ears. He was taking things too fast. Too far. Not for him. But for her. The doc was fragile, both emotionally and physically. To take her to bed and make love with her now would be taking advantage of her weakened emotional state, something he feared she'd regret. If not by morning, eventually.

Lowering her slowly back to her feet, he framed a hand at her face and slowly forced her head back to look at her. Her face remained tipped up to his, her eyes shuttered closed, her lips moist and slightly parted. He felt the thrum of her pulse in the arms wound around his neck, the warmth of her breath against his chin. As he stared, mesmerized by her beauty, her lids lifted slowly, as if weighted, and her gaze met his. He saw the passion that smoked her blue eyes, as well as the wonder.

Aroused by one and humbled by the other, he swept the pad of his thumb beneath her eye. ''That's why I was afraid someone might come gunning for me. I wanted to kiss you and was afraid I had no right.''

And he was afraid, too, if she kept looking at him like she was now, he'd wind up doing more than kiss her. Knowing that, he bussed a quick kiss on the tip of her nose. "We better get inside before the mosquitos carry us away."

Nodding, she slowly drew her arms from around his neck. Before she could move away completely, he caught her hand in his. "Doc?"

She looked up at him expectantly. "Yes?"

"Last night I slept with you. Held you. I can't do that tonight. Not without making love with you."

She ducked her head, her blush turning the passion that already stained her cheeks a brighter red. "I—I understand."

He placed a knuckle beneath her chin and lifted it up. "Do you?" He shook his head. "I don't know that you do. Last night when I crawled into bed with you, I had no intention of touching you. Figured I'd be up and gone before you ever woke up and you'd never know I was there." He shook his head again, then teased her with a smile. "But that was before I knew you were a bed hog."

Her mouth dropped open. "A bed hog!"

"Yep. I wasn't in bed with you for more than ten minutes before you had me hanging by my fingernails off the side."

"I did not!" she cried indignantly, trying to pull away.

He hooked an arm behind her waist, refusing to let her go. "I'm afraid you did, which left me with only two choices. Wrap my arms around you and hang on for dear life, or hit the floor. Since you were a sight softer than the floor, I decided to hang on to you."

When she realized that he was teasing her, she

pushed at his chest. "Serves you right for sneaking into bed with me," she said, hiding a smile.

He caught her hands and held them against his chest, the teasing melting from his eyes. "Doc?"

She grew still, her breath catching at the huskiness in his voice. "Yes?"

"Tonight…lock the door."

Woodrow had told her to lock the door, but Elizabeth hadn't. Not yet. After she'd left him, she'd dressed for bed, and now stood before the closed bedroom door, her fingers poised over the locking mechanism, wavering uncertainly, knowing he was on the other side probably waiting and listening for the click.

Why had he made the request? she wondered. Or had he meant the statement as a warning? He'd made it clear he was attracted to her. Perhaps he'd said what he had because he didn't trust himself to remain in the other room if the door between them wasn't locked.

Or maybe, in making the request, he was leaving the decision of whether or not they became lovers up to her to make.

She drew her hand slowly away from the lock. The attraction wasn't all one-sided. She was attracted to Woodrow as well. But she knew the dangers of entering into a new relationship so soon after ending another. Rebounding. She was familiar enough with the term to know it had a name, as well as a support group. She'd studied about it in one of the many psychology courses she'd taken, even moderated group sessions for women who had suffered its pitfalls.

Was she transferring her feelings for Ted to Woodrow? she asked herself honestly. Was she using Woodrow to fill the void Ted had left in her life? Groaning, she pressed her forehead to the door. What void? Until Woodrow asked her tonight if she had a boyfriend, she hadn't even thought about Ted since she'd given him back his ring. To be honest, she hadn't had time to think about him. Within hours of his leaving, she'd left for Tanner's Crossing with Woodrow.

Woodrow.

She slowly lifted her head, picturing him on the other side of the door, stretched out on the sofa. She laid her palm against the wood, aching to touch him. He had been so kind to her. Offering her his comfort, his understanding. She couldn't imagine Ted offering her either of those things. And Ted certainly would never have insisted upon driving her to the cemetery, as Woodrow had, or even going along with her, for that matter. He would have considered the trip foolish, a waste of both his and her time, and her reasons for making the trip absurd.

But Woodrow had understood her desire to see the place where her sister was buried, her need to come to terms with her past. She'd refused his initial offer to accompany her to the grave site, but he'd followed her anyway, offering her his comfort, sharing with her his strength, when she'd given in to her grief. Even now she could feel the weight of his hand settling on her shoulder as he'd knelt behind her, the surge of warmth and power that had passed from him to her at his touch.

Was it the comfort she yearned for and not the man? she wondered uneasily. At the moment, she feared her emotions were too raw, too chaotic, to trust them.

She reached for the lock and turned it.

Until she was certain of her feelings, she wouldn't become physically involved with Woodrow. She cared too much for him to use him to satisfy her own selfish needs.

Woodrow had stripped down to his jeans and was sitting on the edge of the sofa when he heard the click of the lock. At the sound, he dropped his face to his hands, stifling his moan of disappointment. He'd told her to lock the door. Even made it clear why she should lock it.

But, damn, he'd hoped she'd ignore his warning. Prayed she'd wanted him as badly as he wanted her. With a sigh of resignation, he stood and stripped off his jeans, then stretched out on the sofa and flung an arm across his eyes.

Something cold and wet bumped his arm and Woodrow lifted it to find Blue sitting beside the sofa, her brown eyes soft with pleading.

"Okay, you big mutt," he said and turned onto his side, making room for Blue on the sofa beside him. Wrapping an arm around his dog, he closed his eyes again.

But even Blue, who had shared his bed with him for the last three years, couldn't ease the loneliness that weighed on Woodrow's heart.

Woodrow flipped open his eyes, blinked, trying to figure out what had jarred him from sleep. The telephone rang again, giving him his answer.

Just as he stood, the bedroom door swung wide. The doc stepped into the opening, hugging a hastily donned robe at her waist, her hair mussed from sleep. Her gaze dropped to his boxers.

Woodrow didn't even bother to cover himself.

Gulping, she forced her gaze back to his face. "I heard the phone ringing," she said inanely.

"Yeah," Woodrow muttered, heading for it as it rang again. "I heard it, too."

He snatched up the receiver and growled a threatening, "This better be important."

As he listened, the anger drained from his face.

"How high is her fever?" he asked, then blew out a breath at the response he received. "Man. The kid's burnin' up."

Sure that the call was about her niece, Elizabeth crossed to him, her heart twisting to a knot in her chest. He glanced up at her, said, "I'll ask her," then covered the phone with his hand. "It's Ace," he explained in a low voice. "The kid's running a temperature of a hundred and three. Their family doctor's out of town and Ace was wondering if you'd mind coming over and taking a look at her."

Her blood chilled at the thought of seeing her niece

again, holding her. She wasn't prepared to go through this again. Not yet. She was only just beginning to come to terms with Renee's death. She couldn't handle anything more. Not yet.

don't have my medical bag,'' she said, grabbing at the first excuse that came to mind.

He reached to brush a lock of hair from her face, then laid his palm against her cheek. ''Just take a look at her,'' he requested softly. ''I'll be with you.''

She closed her eyes, feeling the sting of tears behind them, and searched for the strength she'd need to get through this. She found it in the hand that cupped her face.

She opened her eyes and met his gaze. ''All right. Just give me a minute to get dressed.''

When Woodrow stopped in front of his childhood home, every window in the house was ablaze with light. Taking the doc by the elbow, he hustled her up the front steps and inside.

They were greeted by the sound of the baby's pitiful wails.

''Ace!'' he shouted as he headed down the hall. ''Where are y'all?''

Ace's head appeared in the doorway of the nursery, his hair wild, his face creased with worry. ''In here,'' he called, then ducked back into the room.

Woodrow herded the doc down the hall and through the open doorway. He saw Maggie in the adjoining bath, tending the whimpering baby, who lay atop a folded blanket on the vanity. The mirror above it reflected Maggie's face. Silent, helpless tears streaked down her cheeks as she struggled to soothe the child.

He glanced down at the doc, who stood beside him, her gaze frozen on the scene before them.

"Doc?"

Her eyes snapped up to his. He saw the fear there, the dread. He gave her elbow a reassuring squeeze. "I'm right behind you," he said in a low voice.

Taking a deep breath, she gave her a chin a jerk, then strode for the bathroom. Woodrow followed a step behind.

Ace moved over, making a place for the doc beside Maggie, and she shifted easily into the space.

As she looked down at the baby, Woodrow saw the sheen of tears well in her eyes. She gulped, then glanced up at his reflection in the mirror, her gaze desperate, pleading.

You can do it, Doc, he mouthed and shot her a confident wink.

She looked down at the baby again, then set her jaw and pushed up her sleeves. The transformation from helpless female to competent doctor was something to see. Her features smoothed, her lips firmed, her eyes became sharp, focused. All business now, she reached for a bottle of hand soap and squirted a generous amount on her palm.

"What are her symptoms?" she asked as she scrubbed her hands at the sink.

Sniffing, Maggie dragged a hand beneath her nose. "She ran a little temperature yesterday and she's been fussy all day today. I didn't think much of it. Then, this evening, when I was feeding her a bottle, I noticed that she felt warmer.'' Tears brimmed in her eyes and she pressed a hand to her lips, trying to force the emotion back. "I should've taken her temperature then, but I didn't. I figured it was nothing to worry about. That maybe she was getting ready to cut a tooth. Then, about eleven, she woke up screaming.'' The tears pushed higher, seeming to choke her. "W-we tried everything we could to c-calm her down, but nothing s-seemed to help. Th-that's when we d-discovered how high her fever was.''

Unable to continue, Maggie turned her face against Ace's chest and wept.

Wrapping an arm around his wife, Ace took up the story.

"When we undressed her to take her temperature we saw some spots.'' He pointed at the red marks dotting the infant's upper torso, then looked at the doc. "Do you know what's wrong with her?''

The doc bent over the baby, adjusting her glasses in order to better study the rash. Woodrow and Ace watched, each unknowingly holding their breaths. Maggie watched with tears swimming in her eyes, a hand clamped over her mouth.

"Has she had any shots recently?'' the doc asked as she skilfully ran her fingers along the baby's neck, checking for swollen glands.

Maggie dropped her hand and drew in a deep

breath. "No. It's been at least three weeks since she received her last series."

"Any congestion?"

"A little," Maggie confessed. "An occasional cough. I thought I heard a rattle in her chest a while ago, but wasn't sure because she was crying so hard."

Nodding, Elizabeth picked up the baby, crooning to her as she lifted her to hold against her shoulder. "You can take her to your own doctor for verification, but I think what she has is roseola. Are you familiar with the disease?"

Wide-eyed, Maggie nodded. "Yes." She glanced at Ace, the guilt that weighed on her obvious on her face. "I never even thought about roseola. I'm studying to be a nurse, for God's sake!" she cried. "I should have known." Tears welled in her eyes and she buried her face against his chest. "I'm a terrible mother," she sobbed miserably.

Woodrow saw the doc stiffen at Maggie's use of the word *mother,* then watched the slow force of tension from her shoulders.

"No," the doc corrected. "You panicked, which is what most people do when a child is sick." She drew the baby to her arms and cradled her there, looking down at her. Woodrow saw her chin begin to tremble and quickly stepped in, taking the baby from her.

"Come here, you little devil," he said to the infant and shifted in front of the doc, giving her the opportunity to compose herself before she fell apart again. He lifted the baby up and rubbed his nose playfully against her belly. "What do you mean, giving us all such a scare?"

Her composure regained, Elizabeth stepped back into the circle of adults. "Do you have any liquid children's aspirin?" she asked, once again the competent and detached physician.

"Well…yes," Maggie replied.

"Give her a dose, then some juice. That should help her sleep comfortably through the night. She may run a temperature for a couple of days and you may see more red bumps appear. But roseola is a virus, with no serious aftereffects. It will run its course in a matter of days, then she'll be fine." She turned to Woodrow. "If you're ready, I'm sure Maggie and Ace are exhausted and would like to go to bed."

Elizabeth said nothing during the drive back to the cabin, riding with her gaze turned to the passenger window. Woodrow knew something was bothering her and feared he knew what that something was.

He pulled to a stop in front of the cabin, switched off the ignition and turned to her. "You okay, doc?"

Without looking at him, she nodded and reached for the handle. Woodrow watched her slide down from the truck, then pushed open his door and intercepted her at the hood. He caught her arms and held her out in front of him. "You did good, doc," he said quietly. "Real good."

He saw the tears brim in her eyes.

"I know it must hurt," he said. "Seeing your sister's baby. Seeing so much of your sister in the child's face.''

Pressing her fingers against her lips, she dipped her chin and nodded, choked by tears. ''It's so unfair. Renee should be here taking care of her baby. Not Maggie.''

His heart ached to see her suffer so. Hooking an arm around her neck, he drew her up hard against his chest and held her there. ''I know there's nothing I can say to make the hurt go away. You've got to work through your grief in your own way and in your own time.'' He drew in a deep breath, held it. ''But, damn,'' he said, expelling the breath on a frustrated rush of air. He wrapped his arms around her, squeezed. ''I wish there was something I could do to make this easier on you.''

She slid her arms around his middle and rubbed her cheek against his chest. ''You are,'' she whispered tearfully. ''You are.''

He wasn't doing anything but holding her, but if that's what she needed, Woodrow was willing to hold her all night long. He had a feeling she hadn't received nearly enough cuddling in her life. Cradling her in the circle of his arms, he laid his cheek on top of her head and slowly rocked back and forth. Above them, stars glittered on a bed of blue-black velvet and a half-moon gleamed a soft silver-white, its beam making the cabin's tin roof look like polished silver.

Little by little, he felt the tension ease from her body, sensed the weariness that settled over her, weighing her down. He rubbed his cheek against her hair. "You're tired. Let's get you inside and to bed, so you can get some sleep."

She clutched her arms tighter around him. "No. Please. If I go to sleep, I'll only dream."

He knew by the dread in her voice that her dreams wouldn't be pleasant ones. Stooping, he looped an arm behind her knees and hefted her up into his arms. "Well, we can at least get you off your feet."

He carried her to the stand of trees beside his house and laid her down on the hammock that hung between the trunks of two of the largest ones. Bracing a hand along the hammock's far side to hold it steady, he eased down beside her. After settling, he slipped an arm beneath her shoulders and drew her head to rest on his shoulder. "Better?" he asked.

She snuggled close, laying a hand on his chest. "Much."

Folding an arm beneath his head, he stared up at the sky through the lace of the tree's branches. In the distance, he heard the low bawl of one of his cows. Closer, the lonesome hoot of an owl. He'd always enjoyed listening to the sounds of the night. A symphony of sorts he found pleasing to his ear.

"It's peaceful out here," she murmured quietly.

He lifted his head to peer down at the top of hers, surprised that she'd find it so. "Yeah," he said, and laid his head back to rest on his arm again. "I've always thought so."

Lulled by the hammock's gentle sway, he closed his eyes.

"Woodrow?" she asked hesitantly.

"Yeah?"

He felt the nervous pluck of her fingers on one of the buttons on his shirt and knew that she was having a hard time voicing whatever it was she wanted to say. "What is it?" he asked.

Sighing, she pushed up to an elbow. "I know this is none of my business, but I was wondering...have you ever been married?"

Her question came out of thin air and caught him totally off guard. "No," he replied honestly, then frowned. "Why?"

She sank back down, nestling her head in the curve of his shoulder again. "I don't know. It just seems odd that you're not. You're so kind and thoughtful. So loving. It just seems that some woman would have snapped you up by now."

He hooted a laugh. "Lady, you're talking about the wrong man."

She balled her hand against his chest. "No, I'm not," she insisted. "You're all of those things."

"Well, even if you think so, don't go spreading that kind of talk around. You'll ruin my reputation, if you do."

She tipped her head back to look up at him. "What reputation?"

"That I'm the meanest, most cantankerous SOB in the county."

"I beg to differ."

Chuckling, he cupped a hand over the crown of her head and ruffled her hair. "You asked me a question.

Now I get to ask you one. Have *you* ever been married?''

She rolled to her back to stare up at the sky, her head now resting in the curve of his elbow. ''No. But I was engaged.''

He frowned, remembering that she'd told him that there had been a man in her past, one who wasn't there any more. ''What happened?''

''I gave him back his ring.''

''Did you have a reason?''

''He didn't want me to come here. He thought I should go to Europe with him instead, as we'd planned.''

Which meant that she'd only broken the engagements a few days before. He wondered if she still had feelings for the guy. He wasn't sure why he needed to know, but the question burned inside him, demanding an answer. Careful to keep his voice neutral, he asked, ''Any regrets?''

She didn't answer right away and he thought maybe he'd overstepped his bounds by asking.

But then she looked over at him. ''No. Not a single one.''

She held her gaze so steady on his, he wondered if she was trying to tell him something more. Was there a hidden message there? A *hint?*

But Woodrow had never been any good at innuendoes or verbal waltzes. He said what he thought and expected people to do the same with him. He curled his arm around her neck and pulled her face to his. ''I'm going to be real embarrassed, if I'm reading you wrong,'' he said gruffly, then closed his mouth over hers.

He knew the instant their mouths touched that he hadn't misunderstood. Her arms wound around his neck, urging him closer, and her lips parted beneath his on a shuddery sigh.

Five

Elizabeth squealed as Woodrow pulled her over on top of him, making the hammock tilt crazily beneath them.

Chuckling, he gripped her buttocks, holding her to him. "Don't worry. I won't let you fall."

She unfurled her fingers from the ropes. "If you do," she warned, "I'm taking you with me."

The amusement slowly melted from his face as he stared into her eyes. Reaching up, he pulled off her glasses, then lifted his head to brush his lips across hers as he dropped them to the ground. "I can't think of anywhere else I'd rather be."

Tears brimmed in Elizabeth's eyes as desire swirled in her abdomen. No one had ever said anything like that to her before. Not that she was foolish enough to think it was a declaration of love. She wouldn't trust it if it were.

This…this was so much better.

With his gaze on hers, he slipped his hands beneath the waist of her slacks and drew her against him, his arousal obvious against her groin. She wanted him so badly, yet…

I can't do this, she thought, guilt stabbing at her. He had been so kind to her, so good. If nothing else, she owed him honesty.

He lifted his head to kiss her again, and she slipped her fingers between their lips, stopping him.

"Woodrow," she began hesitantly. She gulped, unsure how to explain her feelings to him. "I—I need to tell you something."

He drew back to look at her.

"You're pregnant."

Her eyes bugged wide.

He lifted a brow. "Bad guess?"

"Yes!" she said, choking a laugh. "Definitely a bad guess. Heavens," she said and pressed a shaky hand to her forehead. "What would make you even *think* such a thing, much less say it?"

Shrugging, he reached to thread a strand of hair behind her ear. "You looked so serious, like you dreaded telling me whatever it is you need to say." He shrugged again. "Pregnant was a better choice than the alternative."

"Which would have been?" she prodded expectantly.

"That you didn't want to be with me."

Her heart melting, she caught his hand and drew it to her cheek. "Oh, no. Never that. I enjoy being with you. More than you'll ever know. It's just that—" She caught her lower lip between her teeth, unsure how to explain her mixed emotions. "Woodrow," she said carefully, "I've grown to care for you a great deal. Whether you realize it or not, you fill holes in my life, big, gaping holes that have needed filling for a long, long time. But I don't want that to be my reason for wanting to be with you. Not the sole reason. That would be selfish of me."

He slowly dragged his hands from beneath the waist of her slacks. "So I did read you wrong."

Groaning, she shook her head in frustration. "No. No. You didn't read me wrong. I *want* to make love with you. What I *don't* want to do is *use* you."

A soft smile curved his lips and he reached up and framed her face between his hands. "Why don't you let me decide when and if I'm feeling used?"

"But then it would be too late!" she cried. "The damage would already be done." Moaning, she covered her face with her hands. "If I weren't such an emotional wreck, we wouldn't be having this discussion."

He pulled her hands from her face. "You're not a wreck. Emotional, yes. But considering all you're dealing with right now, I'd be worried about you if you weren't." He curved his fingers around hers and drew her hand to his lips, pressing a kiss against each knuckle. "What if we both were to agree that we're entering into this with our eyes wide-open. No expectations, no strings attached, no commitments. Whaddaya say?"

She stared at him a moment, then threw her arms around his neck. "I'd say that's a wonderful idea."

"I've got another one."

She pushed back to look at him. "What?"

Smiling, he ran his hands up her sides, the tips of his fingers bumping sensuously over each rib. "Let's go inside."

A shiver chased down her spine at the gleam she saw in his eyes. "That's a marvelous idea."

Catching her under her arms, he lifted her, then swung his legs over the side of the hammock, guiding her legs around his waist as he stood. Laughing, Elizabeth locked her arms around his neck and held on as he jogged for the cabin.

When he reached the bedroom, he laid her on the bed, then followed her down, stretching out beside her. With his gaze on hers, he reached for the top button of her blouse and freed it.

"Comfortable?" he asked as he moved his fingers to the next.

She swallowed hard, suddenly finding it difficult to breathe. "Yes, thank you."

By the time he reached the last button, he'd made a liar out of her. She wasn't comfortable. Not any longer. Her legs trembled, her skin was on fire, her pulse throbbed in her veins. With a reverence that stole her breath, he opened his hand over her lace-covered breasts, then dipped his head to press a kiss in the narrow valley between.

Frustrated by the garment's restraints, he fumbled with the bra's front closure. "I don't know why women wear these dad-blame contraptions," he grumbled, then sighed, his pleasure obvious as it fell open, exposing her breasts.

He curled his fingers around the fullness of the closest one. "Beautiful," he murmured, and leaned to sweep his tongue over the nipple. Drawing back, he rubbed his finger over the moisture and watched the nipple bud.

She couldn't breathe. Couldn't move. How could such a bear of a man be so gentle? So tender? So incredibly sensual? A shiver shook her, and he glanced up. Smiled.

"Cold?" he asked.

She shook her head, not trusting her voice.

Keeping his hand cupped at her breast, he leaned to brush his lips over hers, his kiss as fleeting as that of a butterfly drawing nectar from a flower's delicate center. But when he lifted his head to look at her, there was nothing butterflylike in his gaze. Heat smoldered in his eyes, searing her skin, kicking up her pulse. Her mouth suddenly dry, she wet her lips and he slid his gaze down, following the arc of her tongue. Uttering a low, guttural groan, he dipped his head and kissed her.

No, no, she thought, her mind spinning dizzily. Kiss was much too mild a term to describe his effect on her. He consumed her. Possessed her. His lips hot and demanding, his tongue an unrelenting spear that sought the darkest recesses of her soul. She was lost.

Totally, irrevocably lost. And she didn't care. Even yearned to relinquish her body, her mind to him. No one had ever made her feel like this before. So hot. So needy. So desperate. And certainly never so quickly.

She fisted her fingers in his shirt. "Woodrow," she begged.

He pressed a finger against her lips, silencing her. "My fault," he said, misunderstanding the urgency in her voice. "I got carried away."

She shook her head. "No. No. I—"

He shushed her again, this time with a kiss so soft, so brutally tender, it brought tears to her eyes.

Leaning back, he placed the tip of a finger in the hollow of her throat. "You're so small," he said as he slowly drew it down, tracing her length. "So fragile. I could break you. Crush you."

"No, I—"

Before she could tell him that she wasn't fragile, that she wanted him as badly as he wanted her, he hooked a finger in the waist of her slacks and pulled it down below her navel. He pressed his lips to the flesh just below it and suckled as he eased her slacks down her legs. Tossing them aside, he shifted to kneel over her and opened his hands over her abdomen. The imprint of each finger, the wide span of his palm was like a brand on her skin. With a slowness that had her nerves burning, he swept his hands along her hips, then brought them in to shape them around her inner thighs and urge her legs apart. Rocking back on his heels, he simply stared.

It was all Elizabeth could do not to squirm. She'd never undergone such close scrutiny from a man, never experienced the hedonistic pleasure such close examination produced. Sex with Ted had always been an emotionless act, one conducted in the cloak of darkness and beneath the privacy of covers. But this...this!

With his gaze fixed on the V between her legs, he gripped the plackets of his shirt and ripped open the snaps. Flinging the shirt aside, he reached for his belt. Her eyes wide, her heart a jackhammer in her chest, Elizabeth watched him strip off his clothing, then shift back to kneel over her again. By the time he touched her, she was hot, wet, ready. Crazy with need.

He swirled a finger in the honeyed moistness he had produced with his sensual caresses and she closed her eyes, swallowing a groan as pleasure knotted in her womb. Arched high as he pressed the joint of a bent finger against her center.

She opened her eyes and held out her arms. "Woodrow, please..."

He shifted his gaze to hers, then lowered himself down, bracing a hand against the mattress to support his weight as he guided his sex to hers. "I won't hurt you," he promised, his voice husky.

She flinched, tensing as the satin-sheathed shaft pushed inside, then melted around him on a low moan as he surged deeper, his hips bumping sensually against the soft, feminine curve of hers. Wrapping her arms around him, she rose to meet each slow, careful thrust, her mind dulled by passion, her body screaming for release.

When at last she found it, her mind shattered, her body quaked. She sensed the gathering of the muscles in his back and legs, marveled at the shudder that shook him, gloried in the pulsing warmth of his seed as he emptied himself inside her.

His breathing ragged, he sagged against her, his forehead bumping against hers. "You okay?" he gasped.

Purring like a cream-sated cat, she laced her fingers behind his neck and drew his mouth to hers. "Never better."

Elizabeth awakened slowly and stretched, her body sore but her face aglow from the night spent making love. With a contented sigh, she glanced over, expecting to find Woodrow asleep beside her, but found the bed empty. Her smile turning wistful, she smoothed a hand along the shallow imprint his body had left on the sheets. She shivered deliciously, remembering the feel of him moving against her, the seductive power of his hands as he'd swept them over her flesh, touching her in the most intimate of places, stripping her mind of every thought but those of him.

Her smile slowly faded as doubt crept in. Why had he left without waking her? Was it a sign that he hadn't found their night of loving as satisfying as she had? That he didn't share her contentment? Her excitement? Her joy?

Stop it, she lectured silently and rose to shower and

dress. Don't borrow trouble. She'd go and find him, judge for herself his mood, whether or not he had any regrets. And if he did...

No expectations, no strings attached, no commitments, she reminded herself. Those were the terms he'd suggested and the ones she'd agreed to honor. She stopped and pressed a hand to her heart.

But, oh, how she prayed that his perceptions of their night together equaled hers.

She found him in the barn, sitting cross-legged on a bed of hay, bottle-feeding a baby goat. Her heart softened at the tender scene.

"An orphan?" she asked quietly.

He glanced up at the sound of her voice. A slow smile spread across his face, one filled with warmth and a sensual knowing that sent her pulse racing and chased away her doubts. He tipped his head toward the space beside him, indicating for her join him.

"No," he said in answer to her question. "His mama is in that stall over there. Her teats are engorged, which makes it all but impossible for him to nurse."

As she sank down beside him, she reached to scratch the animal between its ears. "Poor baby," she murmured, sympathetically. "I bet that powdered stuff doesn't taste near as good as the real thing."

Chuckling, Woodrow shook his head. "This is the real thing, all right. I milked the mama and filled the bottle with what I drew."

She looked at him curiously. "Will you have to do that from now on?"

"Hopefully not. After a few days, the nanny's teats ought to shrink down to a size that junior here can handle."

The baby goat butted the empty bottle, as if demanding more milk. She laughed. "Greedy little devil, isn't he?"

He passed her the empty bottle and stood. "Yeah, but that's to his advantage," he explained as he opened the stall door and placed the kid inside with its mother. "As long as he's hungry, he'll keep trying to nurse."

She moved to stand before the stall beside Woodrow and laughed again as she watched the baby goat dart for its mother. "How old is he?" she asked, surprised by the animal's agility.

"Two days." Bracing his arms along the top rail, he nodded toward the kid. "Goats are different than most animals. Seems they hit the ground running straight from birth. Look at this," he said and turned for a wide doorway at the end of the barn's long alleyway.

Curious, Elizabeth followed. A closed gate barred the end of the alleyway, and Woodrow stopped before it, propping a boot on its lowest rail and folding his arms along the highest. "Look at 'em," he said, chuckling. "Just like a bunch of first-graders let out for recess."

Elizabeth stared, unable to believe her eyes. What appeared to be hundreds of kids romped and cavorted about in the enclosed area. Several climbed on the trunk and bare limbs of a fallen tree, obviously placed there for their enjoyment, while others ran up and down long wooden ramps, a square platform at their center, playing their own version of king of the mountain.

"They're darling," she murmured, then laughed, pointing. "Did you see that? The little white one, with the brown head, jumped off the platform and spun three hundred and sixty degrees in midair, before landing on its feet."

When Woodrow didn't reply, she glanced over to find him watching her, one side of his mouth curved in a soft smile.

She tipped her head curiously. "What?"

He reached to wind a strand of hair behind her ear. "I like it when you wear your hair down like this. That bun you wind it up in makes you like somebody's spinster aunt."

Which was the same thing as calling her an old maid, Elizabeth thought, an unflattering term she'd heard herself referred to often enough to believe it was true. She dipped her chin, trying not to let the hurt show. "It gets in my way at the office. That's why I wear it up."

He hooked a knuckle beneath her chin and lifted, forcing her gaze to his, his eyes soft in apology. "I never have been much good with pretty words. Worse at passing on a compliment. But that's what that was." He studied her a moment. "You know," he said thoughtfully, "I believe you've got more color in your cheeks this morning. And the blue in your eyes seems sharper, clearer."

"Heavens," she said, laughing self-consciously. "I must have looked really awful last night."

Smiling, he slipped a hand beneath her hair and shaped his fingers around her nape. "No. Not even close. You looked beautiful. You *are* beautiful," he added, as if to make certain she understood his meaning.

A shiver chased down her spine, as she looked into his eyes, seeing nothing but truth there, sincerity. No one had ever told her she was beautiful before. Not that she thought she was. But the way he looked at her made her feel beautiful.

With emotion clotting her throat, she pushed to her toes, steadying herself with a palm against his chest, and kissed him. "Thank you, Woodrow."

Smiling, he turned and dropped his hand to loop his arms low on her waist. "You know, Doc. If that's the way you respond to a compliment, I might consider passing out a few more."

She pushed playfully at his chest. "Oh, you. Now you've ruined it."

"Ruined what?"

"The compliment. If you say something nice to me in the future, I'll wonder if you really meant it or if you just wanted me to kiss you."

"Oh, I'll mean it all right," he assured her. "I never say anything I don't mean. And as to wanting a kiss from you…" He lowered his head over hers. "I'm afraid I'm going to go to my grave wanting that."

Later that morning, Woodrow and Elizabeth stood at the kitchen sink, with Woodrow washing their breakfast dishes and Elizabeth drying.

"What's on the agenda today?" he asked.

Elizabeth paused in her drying, as if considering, then shook her head. "I'm not sure how to go about it, but I'd really like to find out more about Renee and why she was in Killeen."

"Maggie would be the one you'd want to talk to then. She worked with Renee, plus she was her friend."

At the mention of Maggie, Elizabeth quickly turned away to place a plate in the cupboard. Woodrow knew by the flattening of her lips that he'd said the wrong thing. The last person the doc wanted to talk to was Maggie. Not that he blamed her. Maggie hadn't gone out of her way to endear herself to the doc. Plus, Maggie's references to herself as the kid's mother had to be like rubbing salt on an open wound.

"Or," he added quickly, "you could talk to the owner of the Longhorn over in Killeen. That's where she and Maggie worked."

Her shoulders sagging in relief, she turned to him. "That's a wonderful idea, Woodrow. I hadn't thought of speaking with Renee's employer."

He pulled the plug, draining the water from the sink, then caught up the end of the dish towel she held to dry his hands. "Then let's go. No sense wasting time."

She laid a hand on his arm, stopping him. "I don't expect you to go with me. I'm sure you've got other things to do. But I would appreciate a lift to town," she added. "I'm sure I can rent a car there."

He slung an arm around her shoulders and headed her for the door. "You're not renting any damn car," he told her. "Not when I've got a perfectly good truck and the time to drive you anywhere you want to go."

Elizabeth paused in front of the Longhorn and stared at the building's shabby facade, shocked that her sister had worked in a such a place. As for her, if it weren't for the fact that it was broad daylight and Woodrow was at her side, she never would have dared leave the safety of the truck, much less found the nerve to go inside.

"It's not as bad as it looks," Woodrow said, as if reading her thoughts. "These kind of places always look better at night."

Ashamed of her less-than-complimentary thoughts, Elizabeth wound her arm through his and hugged it against her side. "You probably think I'm a snob."

"No, ma'am. But this isn't the kind of place I'd expect to find a lady like you."

She turned her gaze to the gaudy neon sign shaped like a longhorn that hung over the bar's entrance. "And I would never have expected to find Renee here," she said with a sigh, then looked up at him, as if anxious to make him understand. "We weren't raised like this. Not that we were wealthy," she added hurriedly. "But Mother was very strict about our upbringing. Nice girls don't smoke, drink, curse or run around with boys who do," she said, as if quoting from her past. Shifting her gaze back to the building, she shook her head sadly. "If Mother knew that Renee had chosen to live this kind of existence, it would have killed her."

"Sometimes a person doesn't have any other choice," Woodrow said carefully, then glanced at the doc to make sure his comment hadn't offended her. "Look at Maggie," he said. "I know the two of you haven't exactly hit it off, but she's a nice lady. Has a good heart. She had a couple of tough breaks that left her on her own and without the money needed to climb out of the hole she found herself in." He gestured at the building. "According to Maggie, Dixie, the owner of this joint, gave her the chance to turn her life around." He laid his hand over the one the doc had curved over his arm. "What I am trying to say is that just because Renee worked here doesn't mean she was a bad person. Maybe it was her only option."

Elizabeth stared at him a moment, then rose on tiptoe and pressed a kiss to his lips. "Thank you, Woodrow. I don't know what I would do without you."

Embarrassed, he lifted a shoulder. "You'd do just fine." Slipping his arm from hers, he placed his hand in the curve of her back and urged her forward. "How about we go inside and see what Miss Dixie has to say?''

Woodrow tried the door and found it unlocked. Pushing it open, he ushered the doc inside, then followed, closing the door behind him.

''Anybody home?'' he called as he pulled off his hat.

''Depends on who's asking?'' came a woman's gruff reply.

''It's Woodrow Tanner, ma'am,'' he called back. ''Me and a friend of mine would like to talk to you, if you can spare us the time.''

A woman stepped from a doorway that opened off a long hall. Dressed in skin-tight jeans and a black T-shirt with the bar's longhorn logo emblazoned across its front, she looked capable of running a bar. What she lacked in stature, she made up for with moxie. With her flaming red hair teased high and the cigarette dangling off her lower lip, she looked as though she could handle any rowdy cowboy who got out of hand.

She narrowed an eye against the smoke that curled from her cigarette's tip and studied Woodrow.

''It's a damn good thing you didn't lie about who you are,'' she said in a whiskey-rough voice. ''You've got Tanner written all over you.''

Chuckling, Woodrow stepped forward, shifting his hat to one hand and offering her the other. ''It's nice to meet you, Miss Dixie. Maggie's told me a lot about you.''

She eyed him a moment before accepting his hand.

"You boys better be taking good care of that girl. 'Cause, if you don't..."

She didn't finish the warning. But she didn't have to. Woodrow could tell by the protective gleam in her eye that if he or his brothers harmed Maggie in any way, they'd have Dixie to answer to.

"Maggie's a Tanner," Woodrow replied. "We take care of our own."

Dixie eyed him a moment longer, then gave her a chin a decisive jerk, as if Woodrow had passed some kind of test. "That's what family is for," she stated, then shifted her gaze to Elizabeth. "You don't have to tell me who you are," she said. "You're Star's sister."

"Renee," the doc corrected automatically, then peered at Dixie curiously. "How did you know who I am?"

Dixie waved them toward her office. "For one thing, you look like her," she said, leading the way inside. She dropped down on the chair behind a desk littered with paper and snubbed out her cigarette in an ashtray already overflowing with butts, then reared back and laced her fingers over her stomach. "For another, Maggie told me you were in town."

By the purse of her lips, Woodrow suspected that Maggie had shared with Dixie her fear that Elizabeth would take Laura away. A weaker woman would've cowed beneath the fierceness in Dixie's gaze. To Woodrow's surprise—and delight—the doc jutted her chin and met Dixie's gaze squarely.

"I assure you my purpose in coming here is not to do anyone harm."

"Then why are you here?" Dixie shot back.

Though her gaze never wavered, Woodrow detected the slight tremble in the fingers the doc held on her lap.

"I had hoped you might be able to tell me something about my sister."

"She was *your* sister," Dixie replied acidly. "I'd think you'd know more about her than me."

The doc dipped her chin at the verbal attack, gulped. But when she lifted her head, there was fire in her eyes.

"Renee—or Star as you knew her—severed all ties to her family a long time ago. The last time I saw her was five years ago, when she came home for our mother's funeral. I would like to tell you that she came out of love for our mother or, at the very least, respect." Her chin trembled and she set her jaw, against the pain the memories drew, before continuing on. "But her only reason in coming was to claim her portion of our mother's estate."

Woodrow wasn't sure, but he thought he detected a softening in Dixie's eyes. But the old bird was determined to keep anyone from knowing she had a tender side.

"So what do you want to know?" she asked gruffly.

Elizabeth lifted her hands helplessly. "Anything you can tell me. Where she lived. Who her friends were. What her life was like. Why she moved here. Anything.''

Her expression pensive, Dixie picked up a pack of cigarettes and shook one out. ''Star didn't have any friends,'' she said as she fished a lighter out of her jeans pocket. She stuck the cigarette between her lips, scraped the ball of her thumb along the lighter's ball and touched the flame to the cigarette's end. She inhaled deeply, then blew out a stream of smoke as she added, ''Other than Maggie, of course.''

''What about men?'' Elizabeth gave Woodrow an apologetic look, before turning her gaze back to Dixie. ''I know she had an affair with Woodrow's father.''

''Her and about half the female population in the county,'' Dixie muttered, then waved the comment away with her cigarette. ''If it makes you feel any better, he was the only man I ever knew Star to mess with.'' She pursed her lips and gave Woodrow a look. ''Most women find the Tanner men hard to resist.''

Embarrassment burned through Elizabeth, staining her cheeks, knowing that there was one Tanner man she found irresistible.

''But why Killeen?'' she asked, anxious to change the subject. ''Why did Renee move here?''

Dixie snorted. ''Same as every other unattached female who wasn't born and raised in this town. She followed some soldier here who was stationed at Ft. Hood. She told me she met the guy in Las Vegas and he asked her to come and live with him. By the time she arrived, he was gone, leaving her high and dry.''

She lifted a shoulder. "Whether there's a grain of truth in her story, I couldn't tell you. But it's not the first time I've heard that tale."

Elizabeth sat pensively, absorbing what Dixie had told her.

Frowning, Dixie snubbed out the cigarette and reached for another one. "As to why she chose to tie her hopes on an old cuss like Buck Tanner, she never said, though I do have my suspicions."

"His money?" Elizabeth asked bluntly.

"That, too," Dixie said with a frown. "She struck me as a gold digger. No offense intended," she added quickly, as if fearing she'd hurt the doc's feelings.

Elizabeth inhaled a deep, shuddery breath. "None taken. I'm aware of my sister's faults."

Dixie nodded grimly. "She had her share, and then some. But I think she picked ol' Buck out of the herd for more than just his money. I think she was lookin' for a father figure."

Elizabeth frowned, considering. "You may be right," she said thoughtfully. "Renee was just a baby when we lost our father."

"I've seen young women like her before," Dixie said, speaking from wisdom gathered over twenty-odd years tending bar. "Spend their youth runnin' wild and buckin' authority, then wind up with an old codger, because they think he can provide 'em with the security and love they're starvin' for."

Dixie waved her cigarette in front of her face. "Hell, would you listen to me? I sound like one of them armchair psychologists."

"You'd make a good one," Elizabeth said sincerely, then glanced over at Woodrow. "I think we've taken up enough of Dixie's time." Standing, she smiled and offered Dixie her hand. "Thank you, Dixie," she said, squeezing the woman's hand within her own. "Not only for talking with me today, but for all you did for Renee."

Flustered, Dixie took a deep drag on her cigarette, then rose, leaning to tamp it out in the ashtray. "Don't go thinkin' I'm some kind of bleedin' heart," she warned gruffly. "A girl comes to me and asks for work? If I've got an opening, I give her a job. Believe you me, she earns what salary I pay her. What she does with the rest of her time is up to her."

Elizabeth bit back a smile, knowing the woman was doing her best to hide a tender heart. "And I would imagine you consider each and every one of those girls your family."

Dixie jutted her chin. "When you don't have family, you make your own. Blood don't matter." She thumped a fist against her chest and held it there, her eyes filled with the fire of her conviction. "It's what's in the heart that counts."

Six

With Woodrow out checking on his livestock, Elizabeth had plenty of time to reflect on all that Dixie had shared with her about Renee. The facts were easy enough for her to digest, but Dixie's explanation as to why Renee had chosen Buck Tanner as a lover wasn't. Not that Elizabeth disagreed with Dixie's analysis. She could see how that could happen. As a doctor, she understood the psychological phenomena that would lead a young woman to gravitate toward an older man. It was just that she'd never considered that Renee was affected by the absence of a father. She'd only been a baby when their father had died, would have had no memory of him whatsoever.

Elizabeth stilled, her brain snagging on the correlations between mother and child. Her niece would never know her father, either, just as Renee had never known theirs. Would history repeat itself? Would Laura follow the same path Renee had chosen? Rebellion. Running wild and running away. Would her life end as tragically as Renee's?

Groaning, Elizabeth buried her face in her hands. Stop it, she told herself. There was no reason to believe that the lack of a father in her life would affect Laura in the same way it had Renee. It certainly hadn't had the same effect on Elizabeth, and she'd lost her father, too. Surely there were other factors that played into rebellion, other than the lack of a father figure. Unfortunately, at the moment she couldn't remember a one of them.

Making a mental note to study up on rebellion and its causes, she pushed to her feet and headed for the laundry room to transfer her clothes from the washer to the dryer. Not having planned to stay this long in Tanner's Crossing, she was quickly running out of clean things to wear.

She had just turned the dryer on when she heard the cabin door open. Her heart leapt at the sound. *Woodrow.* He was home. She wouldn't allow herself to examine why simply knowing he was near filled her with such joy, such excitement. She refused to psychoanalyze her feelings. It was enough just to *feel.* To know she could care this strongly for a man, that she could openly display her feelings without fear of rejection or condemnation.

Unlike Renee, she hadn't rebelled in her youth, she hadn't run away and she certainly hadn't looked for a father figure in her relationships with men. But she hadn't escaped her childhood without her share of emotional baggage. She wanted family, the love, warmth and security that she'd so desperately wanted growing up. The same things she had yearned for in her relationship with Ted, but never found.

But she had found them with Woodrow. In three short days, she had experienced more, *felt* more than she had during the entire three years she'd spent with Ted.

Was she falling in love?

She pressed a hand to her heart, the realization that she might be so sharp, so shocking, it was a physical pain in her chest.

No, she told herself. She couldn't be.

Or could she…?

"Doc? Where are you?"

She jumped at the sound of his voice. "I'll be right there," she called, then drew in a deep breath, taking a moment to compose herself before going to the den. She found him sitting on the edge of the sofa, stooped over, pulling off his socks, his boots lying on the floor at his feet.

Her heart melted at the sight. "Hi."

He looked up and smiled. "Hi, yourself." He stood and unbuttoned his shirt, his gaze on hers. "Did you get bored while I was gone?"

She shook her head, her mouth going dry as she watched him tug his shirttail from the waist of his jeans and shrug it off. He was so…virile. So unbelievably, incredibly male. She wanted to touch him.

Everywhere. She wanted to splay her palms over the wide breadth of his chest, tunnel her fingers through the dark hair that curled there, rake her thumbs over his nipples and watch them peak. She wanted to shape her hands over the corded muscles in his arms, his thighs, knead them in the firm, paler flesh of his buttocks. And she wanted to taste him. Not just his mouth. Though she could spend hours there alone. She wanted to know the flavor of his skin, sweep her tongue along its surface and discover the different textures, the varying contours.

She curled her fingers into her palms, her nails cutting deep, unable to believe she was having such carnal thoughts. She'd never been an aggressive lover. Never known the desire to assume that role lay dormant and inside her.

But she knew it now.

"Doc? You okay?"

At the concern in his voice, she drew in a deep breath and lifted her gaze to his. "No," she said, the breath shuddering out of her and started toward him. "But I will be."

Her gaze on his, she placed her hands on his chest. "I need you, Woodrow."

She saw the flicker of surprise in his eyes, knew the instant that his body responded to the desire in her eyes. When they'd made love before, he'd handled her with kid gloves, as if she were a fragile piece of china that would shatter at the slightest jostling. But gentleness was not what she wanted from him now. She wanted sex. Hot, sweaty, titillating sex.

With her gaze on his, she splayed her hands over his chest. His body was so beautiful, so strong. Awed by it, she swept her hands over the wide expanse, tunneled her fingers through the hair that curled around his nipples. Unable to resist, she pressed her lips over his heart, then opened her mouth to stroke her tongue over his warm flesh. She tasted the salt on his skin, the heat, felt the wild thrum of his heartbeat, and slid a hand down, closing her fingers around his growing arousal.

He jerked at the contact, tensing, then groaned as she stroked slowly up and down. "If this a dream," he gasped, "please don't wake me up."

Empowered by the need she heard in his voice, she gave him a nudge that sent him stumbling back to sprawl on the sofa, his knees spread wide. With her fingers still curled around his sex, she closed her mouth over his and kissed him deeply, mating her tongue with his, in a dance as old as time. But it wasn't enough. Not nearly enough.

With a whimper, she tore her mouth from his and slid her body down the length of his and placed her lips where her fingers had been only moments before.

She heard the grinding of his teeth, felt the dig of his fingers on her scalp as he knotted his hands in her hair, and gloried in the surge of power that swept through her. Suckling him through the denim, she reached for his zipper.

As desperate as she to be rid of the restrictive clothing, Woodrow quickly unzipped his jeans, then shoved them and his boxers to his knees. Once freed, his erection rose like a phoenix to meet her waiting mouth. She closed her lips around him, teased the swollen head with her tongue.

Woodrow couldn't stand it any longer. If she kept this up, she was going to kill him. Reaching down, he caught her under her arms and dragged her up his chest. He drew her mouth to his and thrust his tongue inside, while he quickly stripped her of her clothes. When she was naked, he kicked free of his jeans and pulled her over his lap, fitting her knees at his hips. With his gaze on hers, he slipped a hand between their sweat-slickened bodies and found her center. He watched the passion build in her eyes as he swirled his finger in the dampness, felt the desperate heave of her chest against his as she fought for each new breath. He pushed his sex against her opening and she arched, her lips parting in a silent cry for release.

With a groan, he pushed inside. Her walls clamped down around him, a velvet glove of pulsing heat. His heart pounding, his skin slick with perspiration, he threaded his fingers through hers and drew her hands up to hold them behind his head.

"Come with me, Doc," he begged as he captured her mouth again. He pushed his hips against hers, each thrust deeper than the one before, more demanding.

He felt the tension building inside her. Felt the desperate claw of her fingers against the back of his hands. She arched high, tearing her mouth from his, and cried out his name, the sound a soft cry of pleasure and wonder that echoed through him. With his entire body trembling with his need for her, he set his jaw and thrust his hips high and hard, burying himself inside her. He held himself there, every ounce of strength he possessed seeping from him as he climaxed.

Weak, he dropped his head back against the sofa and dragged in a breath through his nose. He felt the curve of her lips in a smile against his throat, the rumble of her purr of contentment against his chest, the sensuous sweep of her hands down his arms.

"Doc?" he asked weakly. "Did you take some kind of pill while I was gone?"

Laughing, she nibbled her way up his throat. "Uh-uh."

Puzzled at what had brought about the drastic change in her, he drew his head back to look at her. "Then it's got to be breathing all this clean, country air."

She looked at him coyly. "You're not complaining, are you?"

"Hell, no. You're welcome to take the reins any time you—"

The phone rang and Woodrow groaned at the interruption. Cupping his hands on her hips, he held her against him. "I'm not answering it."

"But it could be important." Stretching, she plucked the phone from its base on the end table and brought it to his ear.

Scowling at her, he growled into the mouthpiece. "This better be good."

He listened a moment. "Now?" he said in frustration, then sighed. "All right. We'll get there as soon as we can."

"Is something wrong?" she asked in concern as she drew the phone away to disconnect the call.

Sighing, he shook his head. "No. It was Ace. All of my brothers are over at the house. They want to meet you."

Her gaze fixed on the road ahead, Elizabeth asked uneasily, "Why do they want to meet me?"

Woodrow reached over the truck's console and gave her knee a reassuring pat. "Don't get yourself all worked up. They don't bite."

"It's not their bite that concerns me," she replied.

"What then?" he asked.

She wrung her hands on her lap. "I feel as if I've been called before a royal court for inspection or something."

He dropped his head back and laughed. "The Tanner men aren't royalty, I assure you." He reached across the console and drew her to his side in an awkward, one-armed hug. "They just want to meet you. Nothing more."

"Easy for you to say," she said miserably. "You aren't the one on display."

Woodrow drew his arm back as he approached the house, noting the vehicles already lined up out front. "Looks like everybody's here," he said, then added. "Even Whit."

"Whit?" she repeated.

"My stepbrother."

He pulled up beside Ry's SUV and parked. "Ready?" he asked, one hand on the door handle.

Swallowing hard, she nodded and opened her door. Woodrow met her at the front of the truck and walked with her to the porch, placing a hand low on her back to guide her.

Before they reached the front door, it swung open.

"They're here!" Ace called over his shoulder, then stepped out and gripped one of Elizabeth's hand between both of his. "You were right on target about the roseola," he said. "Maggie just called—"

"She's not here?" Elizabeth asked, her panic spiraling higher at the thought of being the only woman in a roomful of men.

"No. She took the kid to town to see our family physician. She called a few minutes ago to tell me that he agreed with your diagnosis. Laura definitely has roseola."

Elizabeth knew it was ridiculous, considering she was the one who had suggested that they take the baby to their own doctor for a second opinion. But the fact that they had felt the need to confirm her diagnosis hurt for some inexplicable reason.

She forced a smile. "I'm glad that's all it was."

Still holding her hand, Ace drew her inside. "Come on in and meet the others."

Elizabeth allowed herself to be drawn along, but was surprised when Ace passed by the living room they'd used on her first visit to the Tanner home and led her to the study. The change in venue made her wonder if this was more than a social call.

One step inside the room, she jerked to a stop, feeling as if all the air had been sucked from the space. The brothers rose as one to greet her, five Tanner men, counting Ace and Woodrow, their joined presence so commanding, so overwhelmingly male, it stole her breath.

Ace released her hand and clapped an arm around the shoulders of the nearest man. "This," he said, beginning the introductions, "is Dr. Ryland Tanner."

The similarity between the two brothers was stark. Same raven black hair. Same deep blue eyes. Yet they looked nothing alike. Their individual personalities had molded their faces, making each unique.

By Ry's stiff posture, she could tell that he was more reserved than Ace, almost guarded. She detected an impatience within him, as well. The characteristics chiseled his face into hard lines and darkened his eyes, making him appear formidable, unapproachable.

But he wasn't without manners. He took a step forward, extending his hand. "Ry," he said, indicating that there was no need for formality.

"Elizabeth," she said in return.

"And this," Ace said, moving on to the next brother, "is Rory." He cuffed Rory affectionately on the chin. "He's the baby of the family and spoiled rotten."

Rory gathered her hand between his and shot her a wink. "Don't you believe a word he says, ma'am. He's just jealous 'cause I got all the brains and good looks in the family."

He was handsome, she thought, mesmerized by his

eyes. They were blue like his brothers', but softer, kinder and filled with laughter. Before she knew his intentions, he lifted her hand and pressed a kiss against the back of it.

"Cut it out, Rory," Woodrow warned from behind her.

Rory glanced up at Woodrow, held his gaze a moment, then turned away, muttering under his breath, "How come ya'll always meet 'em first?"

Puzzled by the odd remark, Elizabeth had to force herself to focus as Ace herded her farther into the room and stopped in front of another man. "And this last one here is Whit," he said.

Though certainly as handsome as the others, Whit looked nothing like the Tanner brothers. Where their hair was black, his hair was a sandy brown, streaked by the sun. And he was shy. She could tell this by the way he kept his gaze on the hat he held, his fingers busily plucking at the brim, as if searching for flaws.

When he glanced up, she found herself looking into deep pools, the color of aged whiskey. Charmed by his shyness, she extended a hand. "Hello, Whit. I'm Elizabeth."

A boyish blush stained his cheeks as he shook. "Pleased to meet you, ma'am."

With the introductions made, Ace spread an arm in invitation. "Would you like to have a seat, Elizabeth?"

She glanced quickly around, noting the sofa and

the carefully arranged chairs. No, she thought, this definitely wasn't a social visit.

Choosing the chair closest to her, she sank down. Woodrow quickly slid into the seat next to hers, cutting off Rory, who was headed that way. With a muttered oath, Rory flopped down on the sofa next to Ry. Whit continued to stand, apart from the others, his back braced against the wall, his hat in his hands.

That left only one available chair in the room for Ace—the one behind the desk—but he ignored it and propped a hip on the desk's corner instead. Stacking his hands on his thigh, he offered her a kind smile.

"I'm sure you're wondering why I asked you over this afternoon," he began.

Elizabeth glanced around at the brothers, then slowly nodded. "Well, yes. I have to admit I am rather curious."

Ace inhaled a deep breath. "Well, to be blunt," he said, releasing it, "it's about Laura. Specifically, her future." He rose, dragging a hand over his hair as he began to pace. "As you know, your sister left Laura in Maggie's care, with the instructions that, in the event anything should happen to her, Maggie was to deliver the baby to our father. Since the old man died within days of your sister's death, Maggie brought the baby here and left her with me and my brothers."

He paused in his pacing and glanced over at Elizabeth. "Now this is where it starts getting complicated. Maggie and I love that kid like she was our own and want to adopt her. Would have already, except that there are some legal issues that need to be ironed out first."

Ice filled her veins. "What you want to know is if I intend to sue for custody of my sister's child."

Ace shuddered at the word *sue,* then shook his head. "No, ma'am. I hope it never comes to that. Each of us here," he said, and lifted a hand to indicate his brothers, "has a claim on the kid. Exactly who has the strongest claim, I guess, would have to be decided by a court of law. My brothers have all agreed to allow Maggie and I to adopt the baby and raise her as our own. What I need to know is, are you willing to do the same."

A hole opened in Elizabeth's chest and began to burn. She wasn't prepared for this. Wasn't sure that she would ever be.

"She has no claim."

Every head in the room turned toward the door. Maggie stood there, her face white, her eyes blazing, the baby hugged to her chest.

"Now, Maggie," Ace began patiently.

"No!" she cried, cutting him off as she charged angrily into the room. "If Star had wanted her sister to have her baby, she would have asked me to take Laura to her instead of Buck."

Pain, sharp and debilitating, cut through Elizabeth, ripping open wounds she'd thought scarred over long ago. She stood, her hands and knees trembling uncontrollably. "I'd like to leave now," she said to Woodrow and headed for the door.

Woodrow glanced around the room, his gaze resting on Maggie a moment, then rose with a sigh and followed her out.

Seven

Woodrow had heard the phrase *caught between a rock and a hard place* all his life, but he'd never truly known what it felt like to be caught in that position…until now. Someone was going to get hurt before this business with the kid's future was resolved, and he knew that no matter which side won the battle, he would get blamed for the loss.

Torn between family loyalty and his growing affection for the doc, he followed her into the cabin, wanting to do something to ease her suffering, but helpless as to what that was.

"Would you like something to drink?" he asked, then groaned inwardly, realizing how pathetically inadequate that offer was.

Shaking her head, she moved to stand in front of

the window and stared out, her arms hugged around her waist.

"I know that what Maggie said hurt," he said cautiously. "But you gotta understand that she's running scared right now, shootin' from the hip without thinking first about what she's saying or the damage her words might do."

"Whatever her reasons, what she said was true. Renee didn't want me to have her child. If she had, she would've done as Maggie said and asked her to bring Laura to me." Tears welled in her eyes and she dipped her head, pressing her fingers to her lips. "And that's what hurts," she said, gulping them back. "Not what Maggie said, but knowing that Renee hated me so much that she didn't want me to have her child."

Sure that his heart was going to split wide-open, Woodrow crossed to slip his arms around her from behind. "I doubt she hated you," he said, hugging her to him. "Siblings have disagreements all the time. That isn't the same as hate."

She shook her head. "No. From the time she was twelve years old, Renee made her feelings for me perfectly clear. She hated me, though I never understood why."

Woodrow drew her to the sofa and pulled her down onto his lap, drawing her head beneath his chin. "Tell me about her," he said softly, hoping that in talking about her sister, she would find some kind of understanding, some kind of peace with their past.

Silence stretched out while he waited for her response, the tick of the kitchen clock loud as it counted off each passing second.

When she spoke, her voice was so low, he had to strain to hear.

"She was a beautiful child. Long, white-blond hair and the most mesmerizing blue eyes. Everyone spoiled her. Strangers and acquaintances alike. She had this uncanny ability to charm people into giving her whatever she wanted.

"We lost our father when she was just a baby. We weren't wealthy by any stretch of the imagination and eventually Mother had to go to work to support us. A neighbor kept Renee while I was in school, but she was my responsibility after school and during the summers. I was so young. Caring for Renee was a bit like playing with dolls. I would feed her, bathe her and dress her up in frilly little dresses. She adored me and I adored her. After a while, she grew so accustomed to me taking care of her that she wouldn't let anyone else do anything for her. Not even Mother. If anyone tried, she would throw a temper fit, screaming for me. As she grew older, she became more and more demanding. But nothing I ever did for her was enough. I knew that we—I—had spoiled her and I tried to be more firm with her, more strict."

She shook her head sadly. "By that time, I guess it was too late. She started rebelling, sneaking out of the house, dressing outrageously, acting out. I was in college then, but still living at home. Mother was at a total loss as to what to do with her. I tried everything. Tough love. Grounding. Nothing worked. Then she ran away.''

She shuddered and huddled against Woodrow's chest, as if the memories chilled her. "It was awful. Not knowing where she was or if she was even alive. After about a month, she came home, acting as if nothing had happened, as if she had every right to simply walk back into the house and live there again. Mother and I were so relieved, so thankful that she was home again and safe, that we let her get by with her behavior without suffering any consequences.

"That was a mistake," she admitted regretfully. "A big one. It wasn't long before she ran away again. Then again. Each time she would stay away a little longer. And when she'd come back, she would be even more difficult to deal with, more belligerent. She'd steal from Mother and me, using the money for God knew what. The last time she ran away, I had just graduated from medical school and was living in an apartment on my own. Mother's health was poor and Renee preyed on her unmercifully, demanding money, using guilt to squeeze more and more out of her. I finally put a stop to it by taking over Mother's affairs, thus forcing Renee to have to come to me when she wanted anything. Oh, how she resented that. She told both Mother and me that she was cutting us out of her life.

"In the years that followed, she would contact me from time to time, usually when she was broke or needed me to bail her out of one kind of trouble or another. She never visited Mother again. Never even bothered to call. The last time I saw her was at Mother's funeral. I wanted to hate her. Not so much for what she'd done to me, but for all the pain and misery she'd put Mother through." She tipped her head back to look up at Woodrow, her eyes flooded with tears. "But I couldn't. In spite of it all, I still loved her."

"Are you sure you'll be okay here by yourself?"

Touched by Woodrow's concern, Elizabeth laid a reassuring hand on his cheek. "I'll be fine. Really."

He covered her hand with his. "You could go with me. I'm just running into town to pick up some feed. I won't be gone long."

Shaking her head, she turned away. "Thanks, but, no. I really need to call my office and check in. I haven't done that since I've been here."

With a resigned sigh, he snugged his hat over his head, opened the door, then glanced back. "You're sure you'll be okay?"

She rolled her eyes. "I'll be fine. Now, will you please just *go?*"

"Call if you need me," he said.

"Woodrow!" she said in exasperation.

"Okay, okay," he groused and left, closing the door behind him.

With a shake of her head, Elizabeth headed for the bedroom where she'd left her purse and cell phone.

She was sitting on the side of the bed, the phone tucked between shoulder and ear, listening to her voice-mail messages, when she heard a knock at the door. She hesitated a moment, wondering if she should answer it, then quickly disconnected the call and hurried into the den, telling herself there wasn't any reason why she shouldn't.

When she opened the door, Maggie stood on the other side.

She was tempted to slam the door in her face. Maggie hadn't gone out of her way to be nice to Elizabeth, and Elizabeth certainly didn't feel she owed her any kindness in return. But it wasn't in her nature to be rude. Instead, she asked coolly, "Can I help you?"

Maggie leaned to peer around Elizabeth. "I didn't see Woodrow's truck. Is he home?"

"No. He's gone to town to pick up feed. Would you like for me to give him a message?"

Maggie straightened, meeting Elizabeth's gaze. "No, actually it was you I came to see."

Stunned, Elizabeth stared, noticing for the first time the blotches on Maggie's face, the red-rimmed eyes, and knew she had been crying. Though her heart softened a bit, she lifted her chin, not fully trusting the woman's motives. "Why?"

Maggie dropped her gaze. "I know that I haven't been exactly friendly to you," she said guiltily. "I'm sorry for that. And I'm sorry what for I said earlier. About Star not wanting you to have Laura."

"No, you haven't been friendly," Elizabeth said bluntly, then sighed wearily. "But you were right. I doubt *Star*, as you refer to her, would have wanted me to have her baby."

Maggie sniffed. "I love that baby so much," she

said tearfully. "I can't stand the thought of losing her."

The kinder, nurturing side of Elizabeth wanted to assuage the woman's fears, even offer her comfort. The sensible, rational side told her that wouldn't be fair. Not when she hadn't yet decided what she should do about her sister's baby. "Your affection for the child is obvious," she replied, neatly skirting the issue. "I'm grateful for the care you've given my niece."

Maggie sniffed again, then lifted her head, her face streaked with tears. "I don't know what happened between you and Star. She never talked about her family. But knowing Star like I did, I'd imagine most of the blame was hers."

Elizabeth smiled sadly. "I appreciate you saying that, but I assure you, I made my share of mistakes." She sighed again, her heart heavy. "My one regret is that Renee died before we could resolve our differences."

Maggie dragged a sleeve across her eyes, then gestured to her car parked out front. "I have some of her things. Boxes of stuff that Dixie and I packed up when we cleared out her apartment. I thought you might like to have them."

Pressing a hand to her heart, Elizabeth glanced toward the car, the thought of digging through the remnants of her sister's life filling her with dread. Unsure what secrets of Renee's past would be exposed, she drew in a bracing breath. "Yes, I'd like that very much." She stepped outside. "I'll help you bring them in."

There wasn't much, Elizabeth soon realized. With the two of them working together, they completed the task in two trips. Once all the boxes were stacked on the den floor, Maggie lifted a hand, then let it drop.

"Well, I guess I'll be going," she said.

Elizabeth wasn't sure what made her do it, but she reached out and caught Maggie's hand. "Would you mind staying while I go through them?" Wincing, she shook her head. "I know it sounds cowardly. But the thought of going through her things..." She ducked her head, ashamed to admit her cowardice. "Well, I'd rather not do it alone."

Maggie gave Elizabeth's hand an understanding squeeze. "I know what you mean. When Ace was trying to track down Star's family, he asked me if he could look through the boxes for clues." She shuddered. "Watching him just about did me in."

Grateful for the company, Elizabeth drew Maggie down to the floor to kneel with her before the stack of boxes. She hesitated, suddenly apprehensive about what the boxes would reveal. "I'd imagine there's nothing much of value here," she said nervously.

Maggie reached for a box and opened the lid. "No. Star—" She glanced over at Elizabeth and offered her an apologetic smile. "I mean, Renee. She didn't leave much behind." Leaning forward, she peered inside. "This one has some shoes and some clothes. Nothing I doubt you would want."

Elizabeth edged closer and picked up a sequined

halter top that looked like something a stripteaser would wear. Elizabeth sank back on her heels and held the halter up to her chest. "Oh, Lord," she moaned, looking down. "I can't believe Renee would wear something like this."

"She was a flashy dresser," Maggie conceded, then stifled a laugh.

Elizabeth looked at her curiously. "What?"

Unable to hold back her amusement, Maggie laughed out loud. "I'm sorry," she said, fluttering a hand at the halter. "It's just that is so totally out of character for you."

Elizabeth flattened her lips. "I suppose you think an old maid like me would never dare wear something so revealing."

Maggie sobered immediately, obviously realizing she'd hurt Elizabeth's feelings. "No," she hurried to explain. "It's just that you're such a classy lady and this," she said, gesturing at the top, "is so…so…"

Elizabeth held the top up, eyeing the skimpy material critically. She glanced over at Maggie and arched a brow. "Trashy?"

Maggie bit back a smile. "Trashy isn't exactly the word I was looking for but, yeah, I guess trashy pretty well describes it."

Shifting her gaze back to the top, Elizabeth caught her lower lip between her teeth, as if considering, then shook her head. "No. I couldn't."

"What?" Maggie asked.

Elizabeth quickly folded the halter and tucked it

back into the box. "Oh, it's nothing. Really. Just a silly fantasy."

"Fantasy?" Maggie repeated, her eyes sparking with interest. "What kind of fantasy?"

"It's ridiculous, and I'm ashamed to admit to even having the thought, but I've always wondered what it would be like to be a stripper."

Her mouth sagging open, Maggie sank back on her heels. "No way. Not you."

Elizabeth's cheeks burned with embarrassment. "I told you it was ridiculous. I'd never have the nerve to perform a striptease in front of *one* man, much less a crowd. Besides, I don't have the body for it."

"Who says you don't?" Maggie demanded to know. She hopped to her feet, grabbed Elizabeth's hand, then stooped to pluck the halter and a pair of matching tap pants from the box. "Put these on," she ordered and pressed the skimpy outfit into Elizabeth's hand, "while I look for some appropriate music."

Stunned, Elizabeth stared. "Are you crazy? I'm not going to strip in front of you!"

Maggie rolled her eyes. "You don't have to strip. Just let your hair down and dance." She flapped a dismissing hand. "It's not like anyone will ever know. It's just us girls here." She dug through the CDs stacked beside Woodrow's stereo, popped one into the player, then gave Elizabeth a push, propelling her toward the bedroom. "What are you waiting for? Get busy. This is fantasy time!"

After unloading the feed in the barn, Woodrow headed for the cabin, anxious to check on the doc.

He'd hated leaving her, after she'd had such a tough day. A tough life, for that matter, he amended mentally, remembering all she'd shared with him about her past. All that stuff about her sister... He shook his head sadly. Hard to imagine anyone, much less a sister, putting someone as kind and gentle as the doc through such hell.

As he neared the house, he found himself unconsciously lengthening his stride and realized it wasn't his concern for the doc that made him do so. He wanted to see her. Missed her, even. He'd gotten used to having her around. Small wonder. For a man accustomed to living alone, he'd had her all but living in his hip pocket for the better part of a week. He gave his head a regretful shake. It sure was going to be lonely around the place when she headed back home.

He faltered a step at the thought. *Lonely?* he asked himself, then stopped altogether. Since when was he ever lonely? He was a loner. A recluse. He didn't need anyone, and he sure as hell didn't want anyone needing him. Not friends. Not family. Not acquaintances. He'd carved out his life, one slow scrape of the knife at a time, until he had it sculpted just the way he liked it. He didn't want anyone around messing up things.

He snorted a laugh at his panicked state. What was he getting so worked up about? The doc wasn't staying. Even if he wanted her to, she had a life and a career in Dallas.

One that didn't come close to meshing with the one he'd carved out for himself.

For some unknown reason, he didn't find that thought very comforting. He forced himself into motion again, but stopped a second time when he spotted Maggie's car parked out front.

"Oh, no," he moaned. Fearing the worst, he ran for the house, sure that he'd either find the doc in tears or the two women locked in a hair-pulling contest. He flung open the door and barreled inside, then jerked to a stop, his eyes going wide.

The doc stood on the coffee table, bumping and grinding to some wild jungle beat that pulsed from his speakers. Her hair was down, her feet bare, and she was wearing some kind of gold sequin getup that barely covered the essentials. With the ends of a filmy scarf wrapped around her hands, she was slowly buffing her abdomen with the fabric as she undulated her hips in rhythm with the throbbing beat of the drums.

"What in the Sam Hill is going on in here?" he cried.

Elizabeth jumped at the sound of his voice, nearly falling off the coffee table. And Maggie, who had been laughing and cheering Elizabeth on from the comfort of a nearby chair, shot to her feet. Both women stared at him in wide-eyed horror.

Maggie found her voice first.

"Woodrow," she said, then gulped. "What are you doing home?"

He gave the front door a kick with his heel, slamming it closed behind him. "I live here, remember? What the hell is going on?"

Maggie leapt up on the coffee table and stood in front of Elizabeth, her arms spread wide, trying her best to offer Elizabeth what cover she could.

"Well, you see," she began nervously. "I brought some of Star's stuff over and Elizabeth decided to try on one of the outfits to see if it…fit."

Scowling, Woodrow folded his arms across his chest. "And why would you want to do that?" he asked the doc. "Are you planning on moonlighting as a stripper?"

Insulted by Woodrow's snide tone, Elizabeth pushed out an arm and moved Maggie aside, still riding an adrenalin high from her erotic dancing. "I might," she said defiantly, planting her hands on her hips. "Maggie seems to think I have the talent to make it as a stripper."

The notion was so ridiculous, Woodrow wanted to laugh, but couldn't. Not with the doc standing there in front of him, her chest swelled up like a wet hen, her breasts all but popping out of the sequin top. He gulped, opened his mouth to speak, then closed it to gulp again.

Realizing her effect on him, Elizabeth leaned to loop the scarf around his neck, making sure she gave him a good look at her wares in the process.

"What do you think, Woodrow?" she asked in a sultry voice. "Could I make it as stripper?"

Maggie cleared her throat, as if to remind them that she was there. When neither Woodrow or Elizabeth responded, she mumbled an embarrassed, "I'd better go," hopped down from the table and made a beeline for the front door. "See you guys later."

The door opened, then slammed shut behind her.

Woodrow didn't move. Couldn't.

"What's wrong, Woodrow?" Elizabeth teased. "Cat got your tongue?"

With a growl, he grabbed her and lifted her down, holding her against him as he strode for the bedroom. "If there's a cat in the room, it's you."

Elizabeth drew her nails playfully down his face. "Meow," she purred.

Woodrow tossed her roughly onto the bed, then dove in after her. Pleased with herself—and him—Elizabeth wound her arms around his neck. "You never answered my question. Would I make a good stripper?"

He hooked a finger in the thin band of sequins that secured the halter between her breasts. "I don't know," he said, his voice dropping an octave. "Let's see."

He ripped off the top, making Elizabeth shriek, then dipped his head and captured a breast. Melting on a moan of pleasure, she pushed her fingers through his hair and held his face to her, thrilling at the sensations his suckling drew.

"I don't know for sure," she said, on a breathy sigh, "but I think it's against the rules for customers to touch the dancers."

He rolled over on top of her, pinning her beneath him. "I never was much good at obeying rules."

* * *

The next morning, Elizabeth and Woodrow were still asleep, their limbs tangled, their heads sharing a pillow, when the blast of a horn sounded outside. Woodrow managed to ignore the first irritating blast, but the second one had him rolling from the bed and to his feet with a bearlike growl. Crossing to the window, he threw up the sash.

Blinking sleepily, Elizabeth sat up, drawing the sheet up to cover her bare breasts. "Who is it?"

"That damn brother of mine," Woodrow muttered, then shouted out the window, "What the hell do you want, Rory?"

"Damn, Woodrow," came Rory's astonished reply. "What are you still doing in bed? It's after seven."

Scowling, Woodrow turned from the window and jerked on his jeans. "I'll get rid of him," he muttered, then stomped from the room and out the front door.

Although Elizabeth couldn't see the two men, with the window open, she could hear their voices.

Rory hooted a laugh as Woodrow stepped out onto the porch. "Would you look at you! If you aren't fresh from a woman's arms, I'll eat my hat."

Mortified that Rory knew that she and Woodrow had slept together, Elizabeth bolted from the bed to close the window, before she heard any more.

"Where I sleep and who I sleep with is none of your damn business," Woodrow growled.

"Well, hell, Woodrow," Rory complained. "If I'd known sleeping with the doc was part of the deal, I'd

have cancelled my buying trip and gone to Dallas
myself to sweet-talk her into giving up the kid.''

Elizabeth froze, her nails digging into the wood of
the window's sash. Was that why Woodrow had slept
with her? Was it all part of a scheme to persuade her
to sign over her rights to her niece? Scenes from their
time together flashed through her mind. Woodrow in
the parking lot at her office, telling her that Ace and
Maggie wanted to adopt the baby. Him holding her
while she cried, after she'd seen her niece for the first
time. Him asking her if she'd decided what she
wanted to do about the baby yet. Him carrying her to
his bed and making love with her.

Was it all tied together in some way?

She lowered the window, then stumbled to the
bathroom, her knees like rubber, her mind numb. She
twisted on the shower faucet and stepped beneath the
water, without waiting for it to warm.

But she didn't notice the chilling spray. Rory's
comment had already chilled her to the bone.

When Elizabeth stepped from the bathroom, her
wet hair wrapped in a towel, Woodrow was sitting on
the edge of the bed, tugging on his boots.

Without looking up, he said, ''I've got to go over
to the Bar T and help Ace and the others round up
some cattle. Somebody lost control of their car last
night and tore up about a half mile of fence. The cattle
are scattered from there to kingdom come.''

He stood and stomped his foot into the boot as he
jerked down his zipper and tucked his shirttail into

the waist of his jeans. The action was so manly, so incredibly intimate, Elizabeth turned away, furious with herself for still wanting him.

"How long will you be gone?" she asked, trying her best to keep the anger and hurt from her voice.

"A couple of hours at best. Longer, if the cattle don't cooperate."

She heard the fall of his footsteps behind her, felt the weight of his arms as he slipped them around her from behind, the warmth of his breath against her skin as he nuzzled her neck.

"You wanna ride over with me?" he asked. "You could visit with Maggie and the baby while I'm out with the boys."

Gulping, she steeled herself against the need to turn in his arms and cling to him. "No," she said quietly. "I think I'll just stay here."

He brushed his lips over the curve of her ear. "Are you sure? I might be a while."

Knowing she would crumple if he kept this up, she forced a smile and turned, placing her palms against his chest. "I'll be fine. Really."

With a shrug, he bussed her a quick kiss on the lips, then turned for the bedroom door. "If you change your mind," he called over his shoulder, "give Maggie a call and she'll come and get you. The number for the ranch is on the pad by the phone."

Elizabeth watched him leave, wanting to run after him and beg him to tell her that what Rory had said wasn't true. But her pride kept her rooted to the spot, memorizing every detail, every nuance. The powerful width of his shoulders; his long, confident stride; the cowboy hat tipped low over his brow.

She wept, knowing it was the last time she would ever see Woodrow Tanner.

Eight

After dressing, Elizabeth made up the bed and packed her bag. She was leaving. There was no question about her staying any longer. That decision was made the moment she'd heard Rory's comment. But before she could leave, she had to finish what she'd come to Tanner's Crossing to do. She had to decide what to do about her niece.

But she couldn't think. Not rationally. Not when everywhere she looked, she saw Woodrow. Sprawled on the sofa, his long legs stretched out in front of him, his hand resting on Blue's head, his mouth curved in a contented smile. At the kitchen sink, one hip cocked higher than the other, his cuffs folded back to his elbows, his arms buried in dishwater, washing their breakfast dishes. And she could see him in the bed, lying on his side, his body curved around hers, his face, a breath away, relaxed in sleep.

With a strangled sob, she ran for the door and outside, desperate to escape him, praying that the fresh air would clear her head and give her the ability to make the decision she had to make. With no destination in mind, she slowed, gulping in deep breaths of air, and forced her mind to focus on her problem. Laura. Renee's baby. What to do about her. She didn't bother analyzing the legal aspects of custodianship. Legal rights weren't what was important. It was the child's future and happiness that mattered most. Above all else, she had to do what was best for the child.

But what was best for Laura? she asked herself over and over, her frustration growing each time the answer eluded her.

When she reached the lake, she sank down on a carpet of grass beneath a shade tree near the pier where she and Woodrow had fished, and hugged her knees against her chest, no closer to a solution than she was when she'd started out. She stared across the water, focusing her mind away from the problem itself and to her options. The first—and the one her heart cried out for her to choose—was to adopt the baby herself. She loved Laura and could well afford to raise the child on her own. But in order to do that, she would need to continue her medical practice, which would mean hiring a nanny to care for the baby while she was away from home. The thought of leaving Laura with a stranger held little appeal and rang too true of her own youth, when her mother had been forced to work outside the home, leaving her and Renee alone.

The second option was to sign over her rights and allow Ace and Maggie to adopt the baby. Tears swelled in her throat at the thought. Where would she ever find the courage to sign away her rights to her niece? How could she turn her back and walk away from the only family she had left in the world? In doing so, she would sever her last link with her sister. The one, thin connection Renee had left behind. Her heart breaking at the thought, she dropped her forehead to her knees and wept.

"Elizabeth?"

Her name was spoken so softly, it took hearing it a second time for Elizabeth to realize that she wasn't alone. She lifted her head and found Maggie standing in front of her, peering at her curiously. She had her arms wrapped loosely around Laura, who was nestled in an infant carrier strapped to her front.

She quickly scraped the heels of her hands across her cheeks, wiping away the tears. "I'm sorry. I didn't hear you come up."

Maggie sank down on the grass beside Elizabeth and reached to lay a hand on Elizabeth's arm. "Is something wrong?" she asked in concern.

Fresh tears brimmed in Elizabeth's eyes. "No," she lied, shaking her head. "I'm fine."

Maggie narrowed her eyes. "Did you and Woodrow have a spat?" she asked suspiciously, then huffed a breath. "That's it, isn't it? I swear I'll knock a knot on his head myself, if he's done something to hurt you."

Elizabeth sputtered a laugh, imagining the spunky redhead going to battle for her against a mountain like Woodrow. "No," she said, blotting the tears from the corners of her eyes. "It's nothing like that."

"Then what?" Maggie demanded to know. "You're obviously upset about something."

Smiling softly at the sleeping baby, Elizabeth cupped a hand over the soft curls on the infant's head, then glanced up at Maggie. "May I hold her?"

Maggie lifted the baby from the carrier. "Well, of course you can. You're her aunt."

Aunt, Elizabeth thought as she drew the sleeping infant to cradle her in her arms. "She looks so peaceful," she whispered. "Like a little angel."

Maggie scooted close, her shoulder pressed against Elizabeth's as she smiled down at the baby. "She is an angel," she agreed, then bumped her shoulder against Elizabeth's and added wryly, "but, believe me, she's not so angelic when she's wet or hungry."

Elizabeth chuckled softly. "She came by that honestly. When Renee was a baby, she was the same way. As long as she was dry and her tummy was full, she was happy as could be. But when she wasn't, the entire neighborhood knew about it."

Maggie laughed. "I know just what you mean. Laura's got a set of lungs on her that would put a banshee to shame."

Elizabeth sighed, her heart flooded with memories.

"I always hated it when Renee would cry, and would do anything to make her stop."

"Y'all must have been very close."

Tears welled and Elizabeth could only nod. "Once. But that was a long time ago."

Maggie slipped her arm around Elizabeth's shoulders and hugged her to her side. "I don't know what went wrong between you two, but Renee loved you. I just know she did. If she hadn't, she wouldn't have named her baby after you."

Elizabeth whipped her head around to stare. "What?"

Maggie drew back to look at her. "You didn't know? Laura's full name is Laura Elizabeth. After you," she added, as if to make sure Elizabeth understood the connection.

Stunned, Elizabeth shook her head. "No. I had no idea."

"See?" Maggie said brightly, and gave Elizabeth another hug. "That proves that Renee did love you."

With tears brimming in her eyes, Elizabeth brought her head to rest on Maggie's shoulder. "Oh, Maggie," she said, staring down at the baby. "You'll never know how much it means to me to know that she gave her baby my name."

"I'd have said something sooner, but I figured Woodrow had told you."

Elizabeth stiffened at Maggie's mention of Woodrow, then slowly drew away from her to pluck at a loose thread on the baby's dress. "No. He never mentioned it."

Maggie narrowed an eye. "Woodrow did do something, didn't he? That's why you were crying."

Elizabeth shook her head, but kept her gaze averted. "Why would you think something like that?" she said vaguely.

Maggie placed a finger beneath Elizabeth's chin and drew her face around to hers. "Because I'm a woman," she said flatly. Heaving a sigh, she dropped her hand. "Come on, Elizabeth. You might as well tell me what he did and get it over with, because I'm not leaving you alone until you do."

Tears filled Elizabeth's eyes. "I can't. Really. Besides, he didn't *do* anything to me. I was just foolish, is all."

Maggie folded her arms over her breasts. "You slept with him, didn't you?"

The tears brimmed higher, spilling over Elizabeth's lashes and running down her cheeks. "Yes. But it was a mistake. It wouldn't have happened if I hadn't been so weak."

"He forced you?" Maggie cried.

Elizabeth shook her head. "No, no. Nothing like that. I was a more than willing participant."

Maggie tossed up her hands. "Then what's the big deal? Two consenting adults make love. Where's the mistake in that?"

Fury swelled in Elizabeth's chest. "Because it meant nothing to him. Any of it. It was all a big ruse to persuade me to give up my rights to my niece."

Maggie drew back and stared, her brows drawn together. "No," she said, after a moment, shaking her head. "You're wrong. Woodrow would never do that. I swear, he wouldn't. Yes, Ace and I want to adopt the baby. And, yes, we asked Woodrow to go to Dallas to find you and bring you back here. But the rest just happened. Woodrow would *never* use a woman. He's not like that. I swear he's not."

Elizabeth didn't want to talk about this any longer. There was nothing Maggie could say that would ease the sting of Rory's remark, nothing that she could do that would take away the hurt.

Drawing in a deep breath, she turned to look at Maggie, knowing with a sudden clarity exactly what she should do about her niece.

"I'm going home," she said, "but I need a ride to the airport. Will you take me?"

Her face crumpling, Maggie grabbed her hand and squeezed. "Don't leave," she begged. "Not like this. Please. Talk to Woodrow first. Give him a chance to explain whatever it is that has hurt you."

Drawing her hand away, Elizabeth rose. "No. When we began, I agreed to no expectations, no strings attached, no commitments. At the time, I thought it was a way to keep either of us from getting hurt." She looked away, her gaze settling on the pier, seeing him there, watching his fishing line, his eyes squinted against the sun. Tears welled.

"But that was before I realized I was already in love with him."

At the Killeen airport, Elizabeth purchased her ticket, turned her bag over to the attendant, then rejoined Maggie and the baby in the lobby, where they waited for her.

She forced a brave smile. "My flight leaves in forty-five minutes, so I guess this is where we say goodbye." She glanced down at the baby and her smile softened. "You know," she said, reaching out to trace a finger along the infant's cheek. "I thought deciding what to do about Laura would be really difficult. But in the end, it was all quite clear." She looked up at Maggie and smiled. "I'm her aunt and always will be, just as I was intended to be. But Laura belongs with you and Ace. That's what Renee wanted and that's the way it should be."

Relief flooded Maggie's face, even as tears welled in her eyes. "Oh, Elizabeth, are you sure?"

Her smile growing stronger, Elizabeth placed a reassuring hand on Maggie's shoulder. "Yes. I'm positive. You can tell Ace to send me whatever paperwork is necessary. But know this," she warned, wagging a finger at Maggie's nose. "I'm not agreeing to stay out of her life. I intend to maintain full rights as her aunt, which means I get to spoil her unmercifully."

Laughing through her tears, Maggie threw an arm around Elizabeth's neck and hugged her to her. "You can spoil her all you want."

Drawing back, Elizabeth held out her hands. "Could I hold her one last time, before I go?"

Her lips trembling, Maggie passed the baby into Elizabeth's arms, then moved to her side and slipped an arm around her shoulders. "Come for Thanksgiving,'' she said as they both stared down at the baby. ''And Christmas, too. Holidays were meant for family.''

Family. That was what Elizabeth had always yearned for. Overcome with emotion, she pressed a hand to her lips and nodded. ''I will. And you have to promise to bring Laura to Dallas. We'll take her shopping and to the zoo.''

Tipping her head against Elizabeth's, Maggie hugged her tighter against her side and sniffed back tears. ''I never had a sister. Since you're willing to let us adopt Laura, would you be willing to let us adopt you, too? We could be sisters.''

Blinded by tears, Elizabeth grabbed Maggie's hand and clasped it to her heart. ''Oh, Maggie. Nothing would please me more.''

The Tanner brothers clomped into the house, one by one, with Ace in the lead.

Inhaling deeply, Ace tossed his hat onto the counter. ''Something sure smells good.''

Maggie continued to stir the stew, her back to the door. ''Wipe your feet before you come into my kitchen,'' she snapped.

Frowning, Ace glanced over at Ry, as if to ask, *What's wrong with her?* then shrugged and headed for the stove. ''Hope you cooked enough for an army,'' he said as he wrapped his arms around his wife from behind. ''We're starving.''

For his trouble, he got a stiff elbow in his gut. He

stepped back, frowning. "What's wrong with you?" he asked in confusion.

She swung her head around and gave him a dirty look. "Men," she all but spat at him, then turned back to stir the stew with angry strokes of her hand.

Ace glanced over his shoulder to find his brothers all standing awkwardly at the door, as if unsure whether they dared enter or not. It was one thing to return home and find your wife in a snit. It was quite another to have all your brothers witness the scene.

"Men is a rather vague term," he said, struggling for patience. "Would you like to expand on that?"

She hit the spoon against the lip of the pot hard enough to send splatters of broth shooting halfway across the room, then tossed the spoon down, grasped the pot's handles and spun for the table. "Men," she said again, and slapped the pot down on the center of the table.

Ace planted his hands on his hips. "Obviously you're upset about something. I have to assume by your repeated use of the word *men* that it is the male gender that has ruffled your feathers. But would you please tell me if it is one man who's upset you, or the entire gender?"

She spun and pointed an accusing finger at Woodrow. "Why don't you ask him?"

Woodrow's eyes bugged. "Me?" he asked, hooking a thumb to his chest. "What did I do?"

Pursing her lips, she folded her arms beneath her breasts. "That's what *I'd* like to know. Why don't you tell us all about it?"

Woodrow glanced from one brother to the next, at a loss as to what was going on. He lifted his hands. "Beats the hell out of me."

Maggie took a threatening step toward him. "Well, you can start with Elizabeth," she said, then said as an afterthought to Ace, "By the way, she told me to tell you to send her whatever paperwork is necessary for us to adopt Elizabeth."

"She's going to let us adopt the kid?" Ace asked in amazement.

"Yes," she replied, then focused her fury on Woodrow. "So what did you do to hurt her? And don't bother denying it," she warned, "because I happen to know you did. I saw the tears."

Woodrow couldn't draw a breath. It was as if someone had clamped a band of iron around his chest and was trying to squeeze his heart out through a hole the size of a pin. "Where is she?" was all he could manage to say.

"Gone, that's where. What I want to know is what you did to her to make her leave."

He shook his head. "Nothing. I swear. She was fine when I left this morning." He turned to Rory, who was sporting what promised to be one hell of a shiner. "We were in bed when you came over, Rory. Remember? We'd overslept." He turned back to Maggie. "I swear she was fine when I left her."

"Uh-oh."

Woodrow snapped his head around at the dread he heard in Rory's voice. "What?"

"Was the doc in bed with *you* this morning when I came over?"

"What the hell difference does that make?" Woodrow roared impatiently.

Rory took a step back and to the side, placing Ry between him and Woodrow. "Well, if you'll remember correctly, you stuck your head out the window when I honked."

"Yeah. So?"

"Then you put on your pants and came outside."

Frustrated, Woodrow snapped, "Would you quit shilly-shallying around and say whatever it is you have to say."

Rory dragged a nervous hand down his mouth. "Well, I think I remember saying something about you lookin' like you were fresh from a woman' arms, then something else about me wishing I was the one who had gone to Dallas to fetch the doc."

Woodrow dropped his head back with a groan, remembering all that Rory had said, all that he'd implied. He stood there, still as death, his hands braced on his hips, his head thrown back. When he lowered his head, the eyes he leveled on his brother were filled with murder. "Damn you, Rory," he growled.

Rory bolted for the back door. "I didn't know she was listenin'," he yelled in his defense as he beat a path to his truck.

Prepared to black his brother's other eye, Woodrow started after him. Ace stopped him by clamping a hand on his arm. Woodrow whirled. "Stay out of this," he warned darkly.

Tightening his grip, Ace shook his head. "Fighting with Rory isn't going to fix anything, Woodrow. You know that. It's Elizabeth you need to talk to set things straight."

In the blink of an eye, Woodrow's face turned to stone, his eyes as hard as glass. "Why?" he asked and jerked his arm free. "She was the one who did the leaving, not me."

Elizabeth buried herself in her work, not allowing herself to think about Woodrow or what had happened between them. No one who worked with her—not her nurses nor the two doctors she was in partnership with—suspected that anything out of the ordinary had happened to her during her week away.

But that was because Elizabeth was good at hiding her emotions, her feelings. She had been doing it for years. If nothing else, she could thank her ex-fiancé Ted for refining the talent.

Though she managed to fill her days with the duties of a busy pediatrician, her nights were open for reflection…for remembering. Her insomnia returned with a vengeance, making sleep impossible and leaving dark shadows beneath her eyes. When she did sleep, she dreamed. Though pleasant in nature, even erotic, her dreams held a nightmare quality, in that they were always of Woodrow, haunting her with all that they'd shared and what might've been.

She lost weight, too, pounds her already petite frame couldn't spare, leaving her looking waiflike, in a word, ill. It angered her that she'd given Woodrow the power to hurt her, shamed her to think that she had been so wrong about him. She'd thought him tender, even loving, when all he'd wanted was her rights to her niece.

Feeling the swell of tears, she picked up a patient's chart from her desk and made herself focus on the results from the blood tests attached.

But it was Woodrow's face she saw on the slip of paper, an image so clear, so dear, it made the tears well higher.

Oh, Woodrow, she cried silently, why did you have to make me fall in love with you?

Woodrow sat on the edge of his cabin's front porch, whittling a stick down to a nub, a pile of slender shavings heaped between his feet. Blue lay just beyond, belly down on a carpet of grass, her nose resting on her paws, watching the pile grow. On the ground to Woodrow's left lay another pile, larger than the one he was currently dropping his shavings on, proof to anyone who knew him that he was out of sorts.

Woodrow always whittled when something was bothering him. The process gave him solace, an outlet for his pent-up frustrations, his anger. The act itself kept his hands busy and the pile of shavings he produced a place to bury his pain. But he was sorely afraid that he was going to have to whittle his way through an entire forest of trees, before he had a pile big enough to bury the pain the doc had left him with.

Balling his hand around the knife's handle, he held

his fist against his thigh, his hand trembling as the
rage boiled through him. She'd left him. He'd known
she would. Everyone he loved always did. His
mother. His stepmother, Momma Lee. But it wasn't
always death that robbed him of those he loved. Ace
had left him, too.

It was Ace who had stepped into his mother's
shoes, after her death, taking care of him and his
brothers. And it was Ace who had filled the boots of
their absentee father, a man who cared more about
chasing women than he did about the sons he'd sired.
It was Ace who had held him in the night when he'd
cried, a little boy too young to understand the meaning of death but old enough to feel the pain of the
loss. It was Ace who had gone to his football games
and cheered him on, when their father had chosen to
shack up with some new filly rather than show his
support for his son. It was Ace who had bailed him
out of jail when he'd gotten drunk and busted up a
bar. And it was Ace who had held his head while
he'd puked his guts out afterward.

And it was Ace who had left without a word of
explanation and gone off to find his place in the
world, eventually making a name for himself as a
photographer. Woodrow knew that Ace would never
have left on his own. It was the old man who had run
Ace off. But Ace's leaving had hurt all the same.

Then the old man had brought Momma Lee home
as his bride, though the entire town of Tanner's
Crossing knew as well as the Tanner boys did, that
the marriage certificate the two had signed was more

a business contract than a paper signifying their love. The old man had needed someone to take care of his kids and Momma Lee had needed a name and a home for her son, Whit.

To her credit, Momma Lee had upheld her end of the bargain. She'd cared for the Tanner boys, meeting their physical and emotional needs. Even grew to love them. Woodrow was slow to return that love, but she'd eventually won him over. Then she, too, had left him. Not by choice. A drunk out driving when he should've been at home sleeping off the effects of a night out on the town, ran a red light and broadsided her car, killing her instantly.

It wasn't long after that, that Woodrow had bought his ranch, burying himself in his work and alienating himself from human contact, while steeling his heart against any more pain. It was the life he'd chosen for himself, a means of survival that had worked well for him.

Until the doc had come along.

With a sigh, he adjusted the knife in his hand and turned the blade against the wood, whittling off a thin shaving and letting it fall to the pile between his feet.

The sound of an engine had him glancing up. He frowned when he saw it was Ace's truck barreling down the road toward the cabin. He considered going into the house and locking the door, but figured it wouldn't do any good. A locked door wouldn't stop Ace. It never had when Woodrow was a kid and hid out in his room when he was in trouble. Ace had always found him.

Knowing that, he set aside his knife with a sigh.

"Wondered if you were still alive," Ace called as he climbed down from his truck.

Woodrow snorted. "Like hell you did. I've gone a year or more without seeing hide nor hair of you."

Propping a boot on the edge of the porch, Ace stacked his hands on his thigh and grinned. "Just because you didn't see me, didn't mean I wasn't worrying about you."

Woodrow bit back a smile, knowing it was probably true.

"So what brings you to my neck of the woods?" he asked. "Hunting a baby-sitter so you can take your wife out for a night on the town?"

Chuckling, Ace dragged his boot from the porch and dropped down beside his brother. "If you think Maggie would leave the kid with a renegade like you, you're crazier than I thought you were."

Woodrow lifted a shoulder. "She could do worse. There's always Rory."

Ace sobered immediately. "How long are you going to hold on to your anger before you forgive him?"

"Oh, a hundred or so years ought to do it."

Ace shook his head. "I swear, y'all haven't changed a bit. Grown men, and you're still squabbling and scrapping like a couple of snot-nosed kids."

Scowling, Woodrow brushed scattered shavings from his thigh. "He's the one with the big mouth. If an apology's owed, it's his to deliver."

"I figured you'd feel that way."

Woodrow snapped up his head, watching as Rory

climbed from the passenger side of Ace's truck. His scowl deepened. "If you know what's good for you," he warned, "you'll climb right back in that truck and hightail it out of here."

Rory kept coming, a smile chipping at the corner of his mouth. "Now, Woodrow, you know damn good and well I never could pass up a dare." Two feet from the porch, he stopped and put up his fists. "Come on," he goaded, punching at the air in front of Woodrow's nose. "If it'll make you feel better to go a round or two with me, then let's get it on."

His expression turning sour, Woodrow waved him away. "She's not worth fighting over."

Rory danced a little closer, still punching at air. "If that's so, then why are you still mooning over her?"

Woodrow narrowed an eye at him. "I'm not mooning over anybody."

Rory dropped his hands and nudged the pile of shavings between Woodrow's feet with the toe of his boot. "Then I guess this here is firewood you're putting away for the winter."

Woodrow huffed a breath and looked away. "Funny."

"I'll tell you something funnier," Rory said and stooped, bracing his hands on his knees, to put himself at eye level with his brother. "The doc's a lot like you. When's she upset about something, she has to keep her hands busy or go crazy. The difference is, she knits where you whittle."

"And how would you know what the doc does or doesn't do?"

Rory straightened, with a shrug. "Some things are obvious. In the two weeks since she's been gone, she's knitted three sweaters and a blanket for the kid."

Woodrow glanced over at Ace.

"It's true," Ace confirmed. "They came in yesterday's mail."

Scowling, Woodrow picked up his knife and ran the sides of the blade up and down his thigh, cleaning it. "Lots of people have hobbies," he grumbled. "Hers is knitting. That doesn't prove a damn thing."

"It proves she's unhappy," Rory insisted. "Probably as unhappy as you."

Woodrow snapped up his head. "I'm not unhappy."

Rory choked a laugh. "No, you're the picture of jolliness. No doubt about it."

Woodrow pushed to his feet. "She was the one who did the leaving," he reminded his brothers tersely. "If she's unhappy, it was her own doing. Not mine."

Rory held up his hands. "Can you believe this idiot?" he asked Ace. "He'd let a good woman like the doc slip through his fingers, because he's too damn full of pride to make the first move."

"Like I said," Woodrow repeated, "she's the one who left."

"Have you ever tried considering the situation from her side of the fence?" Rory asked. "According to Maggie, the doc led a pretty sheltered life. Granted, her sister was a ring-tail-tooter, but the doc was so busy trying to keep Renee out of trouble, she didn't have time for much of a social life of her own and has had little experience around men. Hell, if any other woman had overheard what I said that morning, she'd have known right off I was teasing. Men joke about sex all the time.''

"I don't.''

"See!'' Rory cried, pointing an accusing finger at Woodrow. "That just proves my point. You're crazy about the woman. If you weren't, you wouldn't have blacked my eye that morning for saying what I did. Look at this from the doc's perspective,'' Rory went on before Woodrow could deny his claim. "In her mind, you used her. Imagine how that must make her feel.''

Turning his back on Rory, Woodrow faced Ace. "If you brought him over here to try to make things right between us, you can both get the hell out of here. I've listened to about all of his bull I want to hear.''

Ace stood, drawing a sheaf of papers from his pocket. "Actually, this is why I came.''

Frowning, Woodrow took the papers and quickly scanned them, then looked up at Ace. "These are custody papers. Once the doc signs these, the kid is yours?''

Ace nodded.

Woodrow passed the papers back and stuck out his hand. "Congratulations. You'll make a good dad.''

Ace shook Woodrow's hand. "Thanks, brother. That means a lot.'' Frowning, he tapped the papers against his palm, then blew out a long breath. "Listen, Woodrow. There's more. Maggie and I were hoping that you'd hand deliver the papers to Elizabeth, have her sign them, then bring them back here to us. We want this done quickly," he said in a rush, when Woodrow bristled, then lifted a shoulder. "You know how women worry. Maggie's afraid if we give Elizabeth too much time to think about this, she'll change her mind."

Woodrow snorted, seeing right through his brother's scheme. "Yeah. Right."

Rory snagged the papers from Ace's hand. "I told you he was too chicken to go." Swelling his chest, he ran a hand over his shirtfront and preened a bit. "But that's all right, because that means *I* get to deliver the papers to the doc."

An image of his womanizing brother paying a visit on the doc had Woodrow snatching the papers from his hand.

"Like hell you are," he growled.

Nine

With the late start he'd gotten, Woodrow hit Dallas just before midnight. Even at that late hour, the expressway was jammed with cars. Wondering when in the hell these people slept, he bullied his truck over into the far lane, taking the exit that would eventually lead him to the doc's house.

The three-hour drive had given him a lot of time to think. Mostly about what Rory had said. Though he hated to admit that his little brother was right about anything, Woodrow eventually was forced to concede—at least on this one point—that Rory might know a little more than he did about the doc, because what he'd said rang too true. The doc was naive about a lot of things. Especially those concerning men. Whether it was from a sheltered childhood and having to run herd on her wild little sister, he didn't know. But he knew it would have hurt her to hear what Rory had said. She was much too sensitive a woman, too honest and trusting for it not to have hurt. And he supposed he could see how she might have thought he'd used her to get her to sign over the rights to the baby to Ace and Maggie.

But blowing smoke wasn't in Woodrow's nature; he didn't have the patience or the stomach for deceit.

And it angered him a bit to think that the doc thought he did.

As he slowed to a stop for a red light, he rolled his shoulders, trying to ease the tension in them. It didn't help. His shoulders and neck felt as if they were framed from steel rods. He gave himself a shake, trying to relax. God, how he hated cities.

And the city was where the doc had chosen to live.

That thought had him tensing up again. Angry or not with the doc, he'd already decided he couldn't live without her. But could he live in the city, if that's where she chose to remain?

Shuddering at the thought, he tapped his fingers against the steering wheel, irritated by the delay, and shot a glance at the truck's rear mirror. He looked, looked again, then twisted his head around to stare out the rear window, unable to believe what he was seeing. The car behind him was packed with kids, not a one of them looking to be more than sixteen years of age. The driver was using the steering wheel like a drum, beating out the rhythm of a rap song blasting from a set of speakers better suited for a cavernous dance hall. The kid's hair was dyed a putrid shade of orange and cut in what Woodrow thought was called a Mohawk style. He'd seen Indians with similar haircuts in the westerns he watched on TV and figured the style was aptly named. Silver studs pierced the kid's nose, eyebrow and lower lip. Though it was too dark to see, Woodrow would bet his prize bull that the kid's body was covered with tattoos, as were those of the other kids in the car. Smoke billowed from the open windows, and Woodrow didn't think that was a cigarette being passed around in the backseat.

"Weirdos," he muttered under his breath and turned to face the front again, with a scowl. "I'll bet your mothers cry themselves to sleep every night, knowing they gave birth to you."

He froze at the thought, remembering his own youth and the rebellious stage he'd gone through. If not for Ace and a couple of trips to the woodpile, where Ace had tanned his hide but good, Woodrow might've walked on down the path the kids in the car behind him had chosen.

The blast of a horn made Woodrow jump. He glanced up at the light and saw that it had turned green.

"Hey, moron," the kid yelled from behind him. "What shade of green do you want?"

Woodrow looked over his shoulder and the kid stuck up a finger in a salute that needed no translation.

That was all it took to have Woodrow ramming the gearshift into park and climbing down from his truck. He was at the side of the kid's car in four angry strides. "You've got five good fingers on that hand," he told the kid. "Unless you want to make do with four, I'd advise you to keep that middle finger of yours under control."

The kid looked over at his friend in the front seat and grinned, then turned his gaze back to Woodrow. "You gonna make me, cowboy?" he sneered.

It was all Woodrow could do to keep himself from dragging the kid through the window by his ear and giving him the spanking he needed. "That's mighty tough talk," he drawled. He took a step back from the car. "Let's see how tough you really are."

The kid glanced over his shoulder at his friends in the backseat, then reared back and kicked open the door, slamming it against Woodrow's knees.

Caught off guard, Woodrow sucked in a sharp breath as pain ricocheted up and down his legs. Before he could move, they were all over him, kicking and hitting at him like a battering machine gone haywire. A fist caught him on the corner of the eye, another rammed him in the belly, a foot caught him square on a rib. One of the kids jumped him from behind, grabbed a fistful of hair and jerked his head back.

As if in slow motion, Woodrow saw the fist coming toward him, the blade of the knife it gripped catching the gleam from the streetlight overhead. He knew what death looked like, knew the taste of fear. But he also knew he wasn't ready to die. Not when he'd only just started to live. Not when the woman he loved was only three short blocks away. Not when she didn't yet know that he loved her.

He feinted to the left and the knife whizzed by his ear, nicking his neck. He came up with a roar, throwing his arms wide and shucking the kid off his back. With his arms still spread, he charged, scooping the three who stood in front of him up in his arms. Gritting his teeth, he gathered his strength, then heaved, tossing them onto the hood of the car.

Winded, he turned, grabbing for air, adrenalin pumping through his veins, prepared to take on the rest of the gang.

And found himself looking into the business end of a police-issue revolver.

"Put your hands behind your head," the officer behind the gun ordered.

Groaning, Woodrow lifted his hands and locked his fingers behind his head, knowing what this must look like. "I can explain," he said to the officer.

The officer waved the gun, motioning for him to turn around. "You can do your explaining downtown with the rest of these hoodlums. Now spread 'em."

It took over two hours for Woodrow to convince the police officer that he wasn't some crazy psycho, suffering from a bad case of road rage, and to let him go. Of course, the officer finding five ounces of marijuana in the kid's car might've helped Woodrow's case a little. That, along with the fact that all of the boys were members of a local gang that had been terrorizing the neighborhood for several weeks had provided Woodrow with the Get Out of Jail Free card he needed.

It was a little after two in the morning when he staggered up the walkway that led to the doc's house, his body bruised and battered from the beating he'd taken. Exhausted, he leaned into the doorbell, then fell back against the brick wall of her home and waited.

Within minutes, the porch light blinked on, nearly blinding him.

"Who's there?"

He heard the quiver of fear in her voice and smiled at it, imagining the doc standing on the other side of the door with a frying pan gripped in her hand for protection.

"It's me," he said. "Woodrow."

The light blinked out.

He expected the door to open. When it didn't, he pushed away from the wall to frown at it. "Doc?" he called. "Aren't you going to let me in?"

"No. Go away or I'll call the police."

Woodrow groaned, knowing he wouldn't escape a second brush with the law as easily as he had the first. Not when the complaint was filed by a woman as fragile and soft-spoken as the doc.

He laid a hand on the door. "Come on, Doc," he begged. "I just want to talk to you."

"There's nothing you have to say that I want to hear. Now, please leave."

He dropped his head against the back of his hand on a groan, knowing he was at least partially to blame for her refusal to see him. Rory might have set the seed of suspicion in her mind with the lewd comment he'd made, but it was Woodrow who had let it grow and take root with his stubborn refusal to seek her out and explain.

Convinced that he didn't deserve her forgiveness, he straightened with a weary sigh and dabbed at the blood that leaked from a cut on his lip. "Okay, I'll leave," he said. "But could I borrow a bandage before I go?"

His request was met with silence. Deciding that she didn't consider him worthy of even a little bandage, he turned to leave, but stopped when he heard the click of the lock.

He turned back to the door and found the doc standing in the doorway, dressed in a robe, her arms hugged around her waist.

"What do you need a bandage for?"

He touched the corner of his lip again and winced at the sting of his finger striking the raw flesh. "To stop the bleeding."

She took a step toward him. "You're bleeding?" she said, then stopped and hugged her arms tighter around her waist. "What happened?"

Embarrassed to admit that a couple of snot-nosed teenagers with attitudes were responsible for the damage to his face, he said instead, "Let's just say that I ran into a little trouble on my way over here."

She took a step nearer, squinting her eyes against the darkness in order to better see his face. Her eyes shot wide. "Oh, my God, Woodrow," she cried. "You're bleeding."

He nodded his head. "I know. That's why I asked for a bandage."

Gulping, she caught his hand and drew him inside. "Do you need to see a doctor?" she asked in concern as she guided him toward the kitchen.

Woodrow sank down onto the chair she pulled out for him and smiled up at her. "Unless I'm dreaming, I'm seeing one now."

She released his hand and firmed her lips. "I—I'll get my first-aid kit."

Woodrow watched her leave, then tipped his head back and closed his eyes, with a sigh. This wasn't going to be easy, he knew. She was determined to hang on to her anger with him for what she'd thought he'd done to her.

"This might sting a little."

He opened his eyes to find her leaning over him, a medicated swab in her hand. "Do I get a prize if I don't cry?" he asked, trying to tease a smile out of her.

She pursed her lips. "Sorry. I keep all my lollipops at my office."

He flinched as she touched the swab to the corner of his mouth. "Sting!" he roared. "That stuff burns like hell!"

"Better a sting than an infection."

Frowning, he watched her as she shifted to pick up another swab. "I've heard Maggie say that same thing," he muttered. "Is that some kind of medical lingo they teach you in school?"

She squirted a dollop of cream onto the end of the swab, then turned to him again. "No. It's something my mother used to say. Ready?" she asked, holding the swab poised over the cut.

He reared his head back and held up a hand, blocking her. "You already put that on me once. Isn't that enough?"

"If once was enough, I assure you, I wouldn't be doing it again."

Grimacing, he tilted his face up. "Make it fast," he warned. "I'm not into pain."

"Neither am I," she muttered under her breath as she dabbed the swab over the cut.

Hearing the bitterness in her reply, Woodrow caught her wrist and she stilled, shifting her gaze to his.

"I know what Rory said hurt you," he said quietly. "But there wasn't a lick of truth in any of it. What happened between you and me…it just happened. It wasn't part of some scheme I'd cooked up to sway you to give up the kid."

She stared into his eyes a long time, as if searching for something. Whatever it was, she must not have found it, because she dropped her gaze and turned away.

"There's a bandage in the box," she said, in a voice devoid of emotion. "Lock the door behind you when you leave."

She'd almost made it to the door, before Woodrow

could gather his wits about him enough to react. He leapt from the chair and lunged, catching her by her arm.

"Wait, doc. Please," he begged. He turned her around and caught her face between his hands. "Doc, you've gotta believe me. I'd never do anything to hurt you. Never. I swear."

She ducked her head and tears leaked from her eyes and ran between his fingers, burning like acid on his skin.

"Please go," she whispered tearfully. "I've made a big enough fool of myself as it is."

"Fool?" he repeated in confusion, then shook his head. "No way, Doc. You're a lot of things, but you're no fool."

She flung her hands up, breaking his hold on her and stepped back, her face red with anger, her eyes flooded with tears.

"I am a fool," she cried. "I entered into our affair with both eyes open. I even agreed that there would be no expectations, no strings, no commitment." All but shaking with rage, she balled her hands into fists at her sides. "But I fell in love with you. Knowing that our making love meant nothing to you, I was foolish enough to fall in love with you, anyway."

Woodrow held up a hand. "Whoa. Wait a minute. If there's a fool in this room, it's me." He shook his head, as if to clear it, then squinted his eyes to peer at her curiously. "Did you just say that you loved me?"

She pressed a hand to her mouth and hiccuped a sob. "Yes. Now would you please just *go?*"

He shook his head again and started toward her. "No, ma'am. I'm sorry, but I can't do that."

She pushed out a hand, as if to ward him off. "Woodrow, please."

He took her hand and squeezed it between his own. "Doc, we've got us a problem here."

She jutted her chin. "I'm the one with the problem, and I'll handle it on my own."

"No," he corrected. "*We've* got a problem." When she opened her mouth to argue, he cut her off by saying, "Since I fell in love with you, too, that makes it *our* problem."

"Woodrow, I—" She stopped, her eyes rounding as what he'd said sank in. "What did you just say?" she whispered.

"That I fell in love you?"

She nodded, her gaze on his. "Yes. That."

He smiled, feeling the joy in saying the words all the way to his toes. "I have fallen in love with you, though I can't say exactly when."

She wilted, her fingers curling around his. "Oh, Woodrow," she cried softly. "That isn't a problem. Not even close."

Heaving a weary sigh, he took her by the hand and drew her back to the chair. "I'm afraid it is." He sat down and pulled her onto his lap. "You see," he said as he slipped an arm around her waist to hold her, "I hate big cities and you live in one." He shook his head with regret. "I don't have much of a hankerin' to carry on a long-distance romance. In my mind, that's one of those oxymorons my fifth grade English teacher taught me about.''

Elizabeth listened, her heart in her throat. ''So what do you suggest we do about this problem?''

He looked up at her hopefully. ''I don't suppose you'd consider moving your practice to Tanner's Crossing, would you?'' Before she could answer, he pressed a finger against her lips. ''The town's only got one pediatrician,'' he hurried to explain, ''and he's a personal friend of the family, so I know I could get you set up in his office without a problem. You wouldn't have to buy a building or hire any staff. You could just walk right in and start practicing medicine anytime you wanted.'' He paused to draw in a breath, then slowly released it, his gaze on her face. ''Well? What do you think?''

Her eyes brimming with tears, she wrapped her arms around his neck. ''I think that's a wonderful idea.''

Woodrow dropped his head back, limp with relief. ''Thank God,'' he murmured prayerfully.

Laughing, Elizabeth drew his head back so she could see his face. ''Would you really hate living in Dallas that much?''

He pointed a finger at his face. ''Do you see this? And this is after only one night in the city. Imagine what kind of trouble I'd get myself into if I actually moved here permanent-like.''

Her brow furrowed. ''What happened to you, any-way?''

He stretched out his legs, shifting her more comfortably on his lap. "I was attacked while trying to teach a kid a lesson. I guess you could say I was attempting to make a citizen's arrest."

"A citizen's arrest," she repeated doubtfully. "And what crime did this citizen commit?"

"Citizens," he corrected, making sure she knew that there was more than one involved. "And their crime was stupidity."

She sputtered a laugh. "Stupidity isn't a crime."

He gave his chin a decisive jerk. "It damn sure is when they start messing with Woodrow Tanner."

Laughing, she threw her arms around his neck. "Oh, Woodrow," she said, squeezing him tight. "I love you so much."

He shifted her again, this time to a much more intimate position on his lap. "Enough to last a lifetime?" he asked.

She drew back to look at him and saw the hope in his eyes, the need for reassurance, and leaned to press her lips to his. "That and more."

He kissed her deeply, trying to make up for all the time they'd lost, then drew back to look at her. "I have a confession to make."

She stilled at the seriousness of his expression. "What?"

"I wouldn't be here right now, if Ace hadn't sent me."

"Why, you—"

Before she could push from his lap, Woodrow caught her hands in his. "I'd have come eventually," he hurried to tell her. "But I wasn't ready to let go of my anger just yet."

"*Your* anger!" she cried, her voice rising. "I was the one who felt I'd been used."

"Yeah," he agreed. "But you left me. Didn't even give me the benefit of your doubt or a chance to explain."

The anger sagged out of her, her face crumpling. "Oh, Woodrow," she murmured, stroking a hand over his cheek. "I'm so sorry. I should have trusted you. You'd never intentionally hurt me. I know that."

"You do?"

Smiling through her tears, she drew his hand to her heart. "Yes. Inside here."

He cupped a hand at her face and looked deeply into her eyes. "That's where I want to be. Always. In your heart."

"You are and always will be."

Blowing out a breath, he dropped his hand to his pocket. "Now that we've resolved that, we've got some business to take care of."

Her expression curious, she watched him draw the sheaf of papers from his pocket. "What's that?"

"The papers from the lawyer."

The smile melted from her face. "The release of custodianship," she said quietly.

Woodrow knew by the look in her eyes that she was wondering if it was the papers that had brought him to her. He held the papers up, his hands gripping them at the top and ripped down, tearing the papers in two.

Elizabeth's eyes shot wide. "Woodrow!" she cried. "What are you doing?"

He flung the papers into the air. "They're worthless now. Ace had the lawyers draw up the papers, naming you as the kid's aunt. But once we marry, she'll be your half-sister-in-law."

Her mouth dropped open. "Oh, my gosh," she murmured. "I hadn't thought of that." She stared a moment, absorbing that fact, then laid her hand against Woodrow's chest, tears welling in her eyes. "When you told me Renee had died, I thought I'd lost all my family. But I haven't."

His gaze tender, Woodrow caught her hand and drew it to his lips. "No. In fact, you've probably got more family now than you'll ever want. There are five Tanner brothers, and we're just starting to reproduce. Imagine what Christmas will be like in a couple of years. There'll be kids climbing all over the tree and crawling out of the woodwork."

With a sigh of contentment, Elizabeth leaned against him, resting her head beneath his chin. "Will some of those children be ours?"

"You're damn right, they will. At least two, maybe three, if we get started soon."

Elizabeth lifted her head and looked up at him, her eyes filled with her love for him.

"How about now?" she whispered.

Epilogue

September had been unseasonably warm, but October arrived with a bite in the air, a subtle warning that winter was on its way. The wind whined through the trees that surrounded the Tanner family cemetery plot, where four generations of Tanners were laid to rest.

Standing before a mound of freshly turned earth, Elizabeth slipped her arm around Woodrow's waist. "Thank you for doing this," she said quietly. "It means a lot to me to have Renee close by."

"The old man, whether he intended to or not, brought her into this family. It's only fitting that she be buried among the Tanners."

That he would accept her sister so easily within the fold, without ever knowing her and without any resentment for the part she'd played in his father's life, touched Elizabeth's heart. Giving his waist a squeeze, she smiled up at him. "You're a good man, Woodrow Tanner."

He glanced down at her, smiled, then winked. "I don't know about that, but I sure landed me a good woman."

A clanging sound had them both looking over their shoulders.

"What's that noise?" Elizabeth asked curiously.

"Ace ringing the dinner bell. It was his signal for us when we were kids to hightail it for home." With a sigh, he slipped an arm around her shoulders and turned her toward the house. "I guess it's time for the party to start."

"It looks as if they're all here," she said, pointing to the people milling around on the patio at the rear of the house. "There's Rory and Whit. And Dixie!" she cried, recognizing Maggie and Renee's former employer's flaming red hair. She glanced up at Woodrow. "But I thought you said this was supposed to be just a family celebration?"

He lifted a shoulder in a shrug. "She's family. 'Blood's not important,'" he said, quoting Dixie. "'It's what's here that counts.'" Stopping, he laced his fingers with hers and turned, drawing her hand to his heart. "You don't mind that I included her, do you?"

If possible, Elizabeth's love for her new husband increased twofold. She stretched to her toes to press a kiss on his cheek. "No, I don't mind. She's a part of this."

Keeping her hand in his, Woodrow walked on toward the house and the party that awaited him.

He snorted a laugh and tipped his head in the direction of the patio. "Look over there," he said. "Rory's headed for Ry. I give 'em five minutes before they'll be rolling on the ground in a fistfight."

Elizabeth shook her head. "I don't understand you and your brothers. It's obvious you love each other, yet you seem to enjoy beating each other up."

Woodrow chuckled. "I guess you'd have to be a man to understand."

Elizabeth slowed her steps, then stopped altogether, a frown creasing her brow.

"What?" Woodrow asked.

She looked up at him. "I'm worried about Ry."

"Why? He's doing okay."

She caught her lower lip between her teeth and glanced back at the patio where Ry stood, a drink in his hand, talking with Rory. "He seems so unhappy," she said pensively. "When you first told me that he was going through a divorce, I thought that was the reason for his moodiness." Her frown deepening, she shook her head. "But I honestly think it's more than that."

Chuckling, Woodrow hooked an arm around her neck and drew her with him as he strode on for the house. "You worry too much. Ry'll be fine. He's probably just going through a slump right now."

"I hope so," she said, though in her heart she feared that whatever was troubling Ry was more than a "slump" as Woodrow had referred to it.

"Here they come!" Ace shouted. "Crack open that bottle of champagne!"

Elizabeth and Woodrow were quickly surrounded by family, with everyone laughing and talking at once as the celebration of their new life together began.

*   *   *   *   *

Coming in January from
Silhouette Books: a bolder, bigger,
brand-new book in Peggy Moreland's
TANNERS OF TEXAS *miniseries,*
featuring Dr. Ryland Tanner.
Don't miss TANNER'S MILLIONS,
available at your favourite retail outlet.

Silhouette Books is proud to bring you
a brand-new family saga from

PEGGY MORELAND

The TANNERS of TEXAS

*Meet the Tanner brothers:
born to a legacy of scandal—
and destined for love
as deep as their Texas roots!*

Five Brothers and a Baby

(Silhouette Desire #1532,
available September 2003)

Baby, You're Mine

(Silhouette Desire #1544,
available November 2003)

Tanner's Millions

(Silhouette Books,
available January 2004)

Your opinion is important to us! Please take a few moments to share your thoughts with us about your experiences with Harlequin and Silhouette books. Your comments will be very useful in ensuring that we deliver books you love to read. *Please take a few minutes to complete the questionnaire, then send it to us at the address below.*

Send your completed questionnaires to:
Harlequin/Silhouette Reader Survey, P.O. Box 9046, Buffalo, NY 14269-9046

1. As you may know, there are many different lines under the Harlequin and Silhouette brands. Each of the lines is listed below. Please check the box that most represents your reading habit for each line.

Line	Currently read this line	Do not read this line	Not sure if I read this line
Harlequin American Romance	❏	❏	❏
Harlequin Duets	❏	❏	❏
Harlequin Romance	❏	❏	❏
Harlequin Historicals	❏	❏	❏
Harlequin Superromance	❏	❏	❏
Harlequin Intrigue	❏	❏	❏
Harlequin Presents	❏	❏	❏
Harlequin Temptation	❏	❏	❏
Harlequin Blaze	❏	❏	❏
Silhouette Special Edition	❏	❏	❏
Silhouette Romance	❏	❏	❏
Silhouette Intimate Moments	❏	❏	❏
Silhouette Desire	❏	❏	❏

2. Which of the following best describes why you bought *this book?* One answer only, please.

the picture on the cover	❏	the title	❏
the author	❏	the line is one I read often	❏
part of a miniseries	❏	saw an ad in another book	❏
saw an ad in a magazine/newsletter	❏	a friend told me about it	❏
I borrowed/was given this book	❏	other: _____	❏

3. Where did you buy *this book?* One answer only, please.

at Barnes & Noble	❏	at a grocery store	❏
at Waldenbooks	❏	at a drugstore	❏
at Borders	❏	on eHarlequin.com Web site	❏
at another bookstore	❏	from another Web site	❏
at Wal-Mart	❏	Harlequin/Silhouette Reader	❏
at Target	❏	Service/through the mail	
at Kmart	❏	used books from anywhere	❏
at another department store or mass merchandiser	❏	I borrowed/was given this book	❏

4. On average, how many Harlequin and Silhouette books do you buy at one time?

I buy _____ books at one time	❏
I rarely buy a book	❏

MRQ403SD-1A

5. How many times per month do you shop for any *Harlequin and/or Silhouette* books? One answer only, please.

1 or more times a week ❑   a few times per year ❑
1 to 3 times per month ❑   less often than once a year ❑
1 to 2 times every 3 months ❑   never ❑

6. When you think of your ideal heroine, which *one* statement describes her the best? One answer only, please.

She's a woman who is strong-willed ❑   She's a desirable woman ❑
She's a woman who is needed by others ❑   She's a powerful woman ❑
She's a woman who is taken care of ❑   She's a passionate woman ❑
She's an adventurous woman ❑   She's a sensitive woman ❑

7. The following statements describe types or genres of books that you may be interested in reading. Pick *up to 2 types* of books that you are most interested in.

I like to read about truly romantic relationships ❑
I like to read stories that are sexy romances ❑
I like to read romantic comedies ❑
I like to read a romantic mystery/suspense ❑
I like to read about romantic adventures ❑
I like to read romance stories that involve family ❑
I like to read about a romance in times or places that I have never seen ❑
Other: _____ ❑

The following questions help us to group your answers with those readers who are similar to you. Your answers will remain confidential.

8. Please record your year of birth below.

19 ____

9. What is your marital status?

single ❑   married ❑   common-law ❑   widowed ❑
divorced/separated ❑

10. Do you have children 18 years of age or younger currently living at home?

yes ❑   no ❑

11. Which of the following best describes your employment status?

employed full-time or part-time ❑   homemaker ❑   student ❑
retired ❑   unemployed ❑

12. Do you have access to the Internet from either home or work?

yes ❑   no ❑

13. Have you ever visited eHarlequin.com?

yes ❑   no ❑

14. What state do you live in?

_____

15. Are you a member of Harlequin/Silhouette Reader Service?

yes ❑   Account # _____   no ❑   MRQ403SD-1B

COMING NEXT MONTH

#1549 PASSIONATELY EVER AFTER—Metsy Hingle
Dynasties: The Barones
Dot-com millionaire Steven Conti refused to let a supposed family curse keep him from getting what he wanted: Maria Barone. The dark-haired doe-eyed beauty that had shared his bed, refused to share his life, his home. Now Steven would do anything to get—and keep—the woman who haunted him still.

#1550 SOCIAL GRACES—Dixie Browning
Pampered socialites were a familiar breed to marine archaeologist John Leo MacBride. But Valerie Bonnard, whose father's alleged crimes had wrongly implicated his brother, was not what she appeared. Valerie passionately believed in her father's innocence. And soon John and Valerie were uncovering more than the truth....they were uncovering true passions.

#1551 LONETREE RANCHERS: COLT—Kathie DeNosky
Three years before, Colt Wakefield had broken Kaylee Simpson's heart, leaving heartache and—unknowingly—a baby growing inside her. Now, Colt was back, demanding to get to know his daughter. Kaylee had never been able to resist Colt, but could staying at Lonetree Ranch lead to anything but Kaylee's seduction?

#1552 THORN'S CHALLENGE—Brenda Jackson
A charity calendar needed a photograph of the infamous Thorn Westmoreland to increase its sales. But he would only agree to pose for Tara Matthews in exchange for a week of her exclusive company. If being with each other five minutes had both their hearts racing, how would they survive a week without falling into bed?

#1553 LOCKED UP WITH A LAWMAN—Laura Wright
Texas Cattleman's Club: The Stolen Baby
Clint Andover had been given a simple mission: protect mystery woman Jane Doe and nurse Tara Roberts from an unknown enemy. But that job was proving anything but simple with a stubborn woman like Tara. She challenged him at every turn...and the sparks flying between them became flames that neither could control....

#1554 CHRISTMAS BONUS, STRINGS ATTACHED—Susan Crosby
Behind Closed Doors
Private investigator Nate Caldwell had only hired Lyndsey McCord to pose as his temporary wife for an undercover assignment. Yet, sharing close quarters with the green-eyed temptress had Nate forgetting their marriage was only pretend. Falling for an employee was against company policy...until their passion convinced Nate to change the rules!

SDCNM1103